T0022079

MANY THOUSAND GONE

Many Thousand Gone
An American Fable

Ronald L. Fair

WITH AN INTRODUCTION BY
W. RALPH EUBANKS

LIBRARY OF AMERICA

Contents

Introduction

BY W. RALPH EUBANKS

"THE SHOW HAS been put on the road. . . . Three wars, increased migration . . . radio and television have played their parts in creating in Negroes a dissatisfaction with the status quo. The studied efforts to keep them poor and ignorant have broken down under their own weight."[1] The courageous NAACP activist Ruby Hurley made these observations about Mississippi in April 1955, several months before she disguised herself as a sharecropper to investigate the murder of Emmett Till. His murder was only one incident in a long history of white supremacist violence against Black Americans in Mississippi and elsewhere in the South that continued unabated into the 1960s, even as these atrocities galvanized Ruby Hurley and other civil rights activists.

But what if Black people in an isolated corner of Mississippi were removed from the influence of three wars, migration, and modern broadcasting? What if slavery had not ended there in 1865 but persisted for another one hundred years into the 1960s? That premise stands as the basis of the nightmarish tale Ronald L. Fair weaves together in the pages of his first novel, *Many Thousand Gone: An American Fable*. Originally published in January 1965—after the signing of the Civil Rights Act of 1964 but still months before the passage of the Voting Rights Act of 1965—the novel offers a powerful metaphor for Black life under Jim Crow.

In Fair's fable, the Black residents of the fictional Jacobs County and Jacobsville—the county's principal town—have only ever known slavery. They live a life still rooted in the antebellum era, working as enslaved domestics or picking cotton by hand after the advent of mechanical harvesting. Jacobs County is a citadel of the Old South where white people do all they can to keep the Black population isolated within the county, sequestered from external forces and denied access to schooling. Like their enslaved ancestors, the Black inhabitants of Jacobs County are largely illiterate since it is against the law to teach them to read. Those who attempt to flee are hunted down and killed if caught. If they are fortunate enough to evade their pursuers, they are unable to return home because they are wanted by the law. Any escapee who returned to their birthplace with knowledge of the outside world would disrupt the antebellum way of life the county is determined to maintain. But very few manage to escape. As Fair describes his fictional land, "The residents of Mississippi delighted in seeing the white-shirted guards returning from a successful hunt, the limp body of a Negro dragging behind a horse. To them Jacobs County was the south as it should have remained, and they kept the secret well."

That Jacobs County represents the legacy of slavery in the Jim Crow South is made explicit in a metafictional moment early in the novel, when one of the inhabitants of a nearby Mississippi county tells Granny Jacobs, who is secretly sending her great-grandson out of the county to Chicago, "It ain't much better here." Fair confronts the many cruelties of life under Jim Crow, including the lynching of Black men, the serial rape of Black women, economic exploitation of Black farmers, and restrictions on how Black people could travel and where they could live. It is *as if* slavery had never ended.

The isolation of rural Mississippi, paired with a political and racial climate marked by violence, created a culture that made the state synonymous with degradation and deprivation much like that in Fair's fictional world. Large clusters of impoverished Black inhabitants and its predominately rural countryside ensured the state's isolation well into the twentieth century. In 1900, Mississippi was 92.3 percent rural. By the 1960s, when the rest of the United States was only 30 percent rural, Mississippi remained 62.3 percent rural.

As a Mississippi native who grew up during the civil rights movement, I find it difficult to read Fair's descriptions of Jacobs County and not think of the Mississippi Delta, the rich alluvial plain between the Mississippi and Yazoo Rivers in the northwest part of the state, a region that maintained a tightly controlled plantation economy until the mid-1960s. Fair never gives us the precise location of Jacobs County, but it occupies former Chickasaw lands and its Black inhabitants work in plantation cotton fields. The first town north of Jacobsville is Minnott, possibly a reference to the real-life rural community of Minot. These details seem to place Jacobs County in the Delta, in Sunflower County—about ninety miles southwest of Lafayette County, the inspiration for Faulkner's apocryphal Yoknapatawpha.

The Delta's plantation owners played a significant role in shaping what became known as the "Mississippi Plan." This carefully constructed scheme for the disenfranchisement of Black citizens in Mississippi shaped the political and cultural landscape of the Magnolia State, and the entire American South, for nearly a century, essentially the period Fair covers in *Many Thousand Gone*. White Delta residents were until recently extremely proud of the way their ancestors ushered in a second period of white supremacy in the South. In *Lanterns on the Levee* (1941), William Alexander Percy, for example, boastfully recalls how his own ancestors made this happen: "These were men who . . . bore the brunt of the Delta's fight against scalawaggery and Negro domination during reconstruction, who stole the ballot boxes which, honestly counted, would have made every county official a Negro, who had helped shape the Constitution of 1890, which legally disenfranchised the Negro."[2]

In the Mississippi Delta, sharecropping was a successor system to slavery, one that kept most Black Delta residents beholden to plantation owners, who controlled both how much sharecroppers earned and how much they owed. When an owner advanced money or extended credit for fertilizer and seed as well as essentials such as clothing, housing, and food, in exchange for a share of the crop, they frequently bound the Black sharecropper and his family to the plantation with little or no chance of ever escaping debt. The rare Black landowner in the Delta struggled to earn a living under an economic system controlled by the ruling plantation elite.

Throughout *Many Thousand Gone*, Fair weaves stories and circumstances that are an indictment not only of southern racism, but also of northern indifference and complicity. He wants his readers to recognize that Jacobs County has been shaped by economic, political, and psychological forces that are American at their core, not merely southern. Why no one, in the South or the North, has chosen to free the town from the system of slavery that has ruled their lives is a matter of speculation among the county's Black inhabitants:

> "We been born down here where nobody can help us. I kinda reckon some of them white people up north might want to help if they knew about us, but they don't know we's down here. They don't know we still slaves."

"They knows, Granny," a young man said. "They knows and they don't give a damn what happens to us 'cause we just black."

Fair forces the reader to ponder something that was not yet part of the mainstream cultural conversation in 1965: the ways during Reconstruction and its aftermath that Black Americans had been abandoned in the rush to unify the North and the South. Bear in mind that this is a book published during the final year of the centennial commemoration of the Civil War, in a period still dominated by the Lost Cause narrative. In his fantastical world, Fair makes his reader aware that the rebuilding of the Union meant the loss of freedom for the very people the North had emancipated. Northern blindness to the injustices of the South was just as harmful as the actions of white southerners. As W.E.B. Du Bois wrote in *Black Reconstruction in America* in 1935, "The slave went free; stood a brief moment in the sun; then moved back again toward slavery."[3]

Through their mutual preoccupation with miscegenation the creators of the fictional domains of Jacobs and Yoknapatawpha Counties become linked in the reader's mind. "For the horror that the 'one drop' rule excites," Toni Morrison writes, "there is no better guide than William Faulkner. What else haunts *The Sound and the Fury* and *Absalom, Absalom!*?"[4] The white horror of miscegenation evoked by Faulkner finds an opposite corollary in Fair's novel in the delight that the Black inhabitants of Jacobs County take in their Black ancestry: "They were proud not to be white." Indeed, it has become a long-standing practice in Jacobs County to honor the first-born child of a firstborn child because these are the only children believed to be pure of race, given the constant specter of rape of Black women by white men—a weapon of white domination that serves to demoralize both Black women and men. "No one remembered how the custom had started," Fair's narrator explains, "but down the years it had become firmly established, and they continued to celebrate joyously for the increasingly rare first-borns who were genuinely Negro."

Since all Black women in the county have been made sexually available for generations to any white man, eventually the last all-Black child, Jesse, also known as "the Black Prince," is born. Fearing that he will be lynched, his great-grandmother, Granny Jacobs, with the help of other Black people, spirits him away to Chicago, where he joins his pure-blood father, who earlier had fled Jacobs County. The name "Jesse" alludes to Isaiah 11:1: "And there shall come forth a rod out of the stem of Jesse, and a Branch shall grow out of his roots."

It is Jesse's fame as a writer that eventually places a spotlight on Jacobsville, echoing how Richard Wright, who also moved from Mississippi to Chicago, placed new scrutiny on his native state in his celebrated memoir *Black Boy*, published in 1945. As did Wright, Jesse comes to realize that he can use words as a weapon. After a profile piece on Jesse appears in *Ebony* prior to the publication of Jesse's book about Jacobsville, the photographs of Black bourgeois prosperity and respectability accompanying the piece shock the white community in Jacobs County, exposing its false sense of superiority while emboldening the county's Black inhabitants. Things then begin to quickly unravel.

When federal marshals arrive in Jacobs County—prompted by a letter written by the only literate Black person in the county, Preacher Harris—they are viewed suspiciously by local Black folks while the sheriff's office views them with genuine alarm, since the sheriff "had seen the federal marshals in Oxford in 1962 and he didn't want any in Jacobs County"—a reference to the deadly rioting that erupted on the University of Mississippi campus when angry white protestors tried to prevent James Meredith, who was under federal protection, from becoming the first Black student to enroll in the University. In Fair's novel, however, it is the federal marshals, and not the white perpetrators of violence, who find themselves jailed, outwitted by the "vulgar, illiterate sheriff . . . because all the time he had known something they didn't know. He knew . . . he was fighting the same war his great-grandfather had fought."

Significantly, it is not the power of the federal government that inspires the Black majority of Jacobs County to resist their white oppressors; rather, it is the people themselves who take responsibility for their liberation. Fair reminds us that the story of the civil rights movement is largely that of the assertion of Black power and Black determination. Power is not just a negative, coercive, or repressive force that compels us to do things against our will. Disassociating Blackness from societal power masks the ways in which the changes brought about by the civil rights movement came through the assertion of power by ordinary everyday Black citizens, a force strong enough to break the yoke of white supremacy that had long reigned over their lives.

In the novel's final chapter, the character Josh, who once worked for the county sheriff, helps incinerate the homes and businesses of the white minority of Jacobsville after a group of unidentified white men commit horrible atrocities against the county's Black inhabitants. At the novel's conclusion, it is Josh who "waited until the flames had consumed one whole side of the building. Then he casually reached into his pocket, took out a set of keys, unlocked the door, and hurried inside to set his emancipators free."

There are few biographical clues for what shaped *Many Thousand Gone*. Fair once recalled that he began writing as a teenager because of his "anger with the life I knew and the inability of anyone I knew to explain why things were the way they were."[5] In a short personal note accompanying his 1972 autobiographical novel, *We Can't Breathe*, we find a hint of the impact his family's roots in Mississippi had on his writing. "This is a narrative of what it was like for those of us born in the thirties," Fair writes. "Our parents came from Mississippi, Louisiana,

Tennessee, and many other southern states where whites were perverse and in-human in their treatment of blacks. . . . They came north, and we were the children born in the place they escaped to—Chicago."[6] Born in Chicago in 1932, Fair would have found it difficult to escape stories of Mississippi that his father, Hubert, brought with him when he left the state and moved north. Likely, the author still had relatives living in places that bore resemblance to his fictional Jacobs County. By the time Fair published *Many Thousand Gone* in 1965, Black Americans made up about 40 percent of the population in Mississippi. That made the idea of Black power something to be feared in the rural South as much as in the urban North.[7]

In a letter published in the *Chicago Daily Defender* in 1963, Fair wrote, "The racial revolution taking place in our country is a warming and inspiring thing to most Americans. . . . The Negro is fighting for his share of this great country that he helped make."[8] Less than a year later, the events of the civil rights movement in Mississippi were being broadcast daily on the nightly news and appeared in national newspapers. As Freedom Summer volunteers arrived in Mississippi in 1964 to register Black voters, activists Andrew Goodman, James Chaney, and Michael Schwerner were murdered in Neshoba County by a group of Klansmen that included members of the county sheriff's department. Two months later the Democratic National Convention refused to seat the integrated delegation sent by the Mississippi Freedom Democratic Party, revealing the limits of northern support for the civil rights movement. As these events unfolded Fair was at work on his remarkable novel, blending the memory of the old world that shaped his parents' lives with the new world that was rising up before his very eyes as Black Americans fought for racial justice and equality.

Steeped in the era's spirit of revolution, *Many Thousand Gone* reveals how the assertion of power lies at the core of humanity and is a necessary and needed force to secure the basic human needs of fairness and equality. This book—restored to print by Library of America after decades of neglect—reinforces my belief that works of literature and works of memory have a way of renewing and retying our links to the past and the present. For Fair himself, change may have come too slowly. Increasingly disenchanted with American culture and politics, he left the United States for Europe in 1971, eventually giving up a public literary life for a career as a sculptor. But his remarkable novel endures. As the narrative of the civil rights era becomes diluted by time and memory, Fair's fable about an imagined yet real place in Mississippi stands as a literary work that recognizes the ways Black societal power changed America and understands the forces that were necessary to create those changes.

NOTES

1. Ruby Hurley, "Economic Pressure," NAACP Papers (1955), Library of Congress, cited in Charles M. Payne, *I've Got the Light of Freedom* (Berkeley: University of California Press, 1995), 7.

2. William Alexander Percy, *Lanterns on the Levee: Recollections of a Planter's Son* (New York: Alfred A. Knopf, 1941), 68–69.

3. *W.E.B. Du Bois: Black Reconstruction & Other Writings*, ed. Eric Foner and Henry Louis Gates, Jr. (New York Library of America, 2021), 40.

4. Toni Morrison, *The Origin of Others* (Cambridge, MA: Harvard University Press, 2017), 41–42.

5. R. Baxter Miller, "Ronald L. Fair," in Thadious M. Davis, ed., *Dictionary of Literary Biography* (Vol. 33): *Afro-American Fiction Writers After 1955* (Detroit, MI: Gale Research, 1984) 67.

6. Ronald L. Fair, Author's Note in *We Can't Breathe* (New York: Harper & Row, 1972).

7. Black power as an idea—as opposed to the political and social movement we associate with the late 1960s and the 1970s—is one that predates Fair's novel. In *Black Power* (1954) Richard Wright was already wrestling with the notion of marrying a Blackness rooted in the South with the vision of Black empowerment he encountered on the African continent.

8. Ronald L. Fair, "Racial Revolution Is Inspiring to Americans," *Chicago Daily Defender* (September 21, 1963).

MANY THOUSAND GONE

THIS BOOK IS DEDICATED TO

Robert H. Ingalls, the late Alex Wilson,
Mrs. Jewel Coleman, Edwin G. Schwenn,
and my darling Lucy

No more auction-block for me,
No more, no more;
No more auction-block for me,
Many thousand gone.

No more peck o' corn for me,
No more, no more;
No more peck o' corn for me,
Many thousand gone.

No more driver's lash for me,
No more, no more;
No more driver's lash for me,
Many thousand gone.

NEGRO SPIRITUAL

Part One

One

JACOBSVILLE IS A TOWN in the County of Jacobs in the State of Mississippi. It was founded by Mr. Samuel Jacobs, a prudent adventurer who grew up in Natchez, Mississippi, where, with the aid of a shrewd lawyer and a bribed judge, he was launched into a position of eminence by having himself appointed executor of an estate valued at one hundred thousand dollars. Once the estate was in his hands, his destiny was assured.

The only heir to this rich plantation was a ten-year-old girl. Mr. Jacobs sent the child north to school and petitioned the court for permission to sell the property at the best price, and so pay the boarding-school bills. His friend the judge allowed the petition and the plantation was sold to a man, acting as an agent for Mr. Jacobs, for ten thousand dollars. It was then signed over to Mr. Jacobs and a short time thereafter was resold at a considerable profit.

Once this successful business venture had been completed,

he was financially able to manipulate politicians of far greater importance than the local judge. And when the federal government bludgeoned the Chickasaw Indians into signing the treaty of 1832, Mr. Jacobs hastened their departure by leading raids against their smaller villages. His raids served two purposes: one was to clear the Indians out of the territory he had chosen for himself and the other was to kidnap the Negroes who had escaped slavery and found sanctuary among the Indians.

Many of these Negroes had lived with the Indians for years, married women of the tribe and had children by them. These free Negroes, knowing the value of their freedom, fought even harder than the Indians, and in some cases, rather than return to slavery, chose to destroy themselves.

Mr. Jacobs kept only those slaves that were one-hundred-per-cent Negro. Those that were half Indian he sold immediately because he felt they would not take well to slavery.

By 1835 the last of the Chickasaws had moved west and Mr. Jacobs made a claim to the federal government for a great portion of the new land, as indemnification for services rendered in assisting the removal of the Indians. After an official survey, the area was named Jacobs' Section. Mr. Jacobs welcomed settlers and staked them to more land than they could use. He agreed that payment in labor on his own land would be satisfactory. It was a fine arrangement.

In 1836 the State of Mississippi redistricted and Jacobs' Section became a county, the smallest in Mississippi. Before long the town of Jacobsville was founded, and it was from here that Mr. Jacobs ruled his county and prospered until the Civil War began.

The Civil War years were hard on Jacobs County. The land had been without cotton too long, a great many of the slaves were gone, and those who remained thought that they were free. Mr. Jacobs returned home from the war, and with the aid of his only son, Sam, immediately set about putting things in order.

He worked closely with the Yankee officers, and succeeded in isolating Jacobs County from the rest of the world by donating enough land to the state so that all roads in the area, except one well-hidden dirt road, could be detoured around it. By the time the reconstruction period ended, the Negroes who held fast to the land found themselves slaves again, unable to flee Mr. Jacobs and his army of fifty guards who patroled the county line day and night.

Occasionally Negroes were able to slip past the sentries, but someone would always tell of the escape and the guards would pursue them, even into neighboring states, until they were apprehended. The residents of Mississippi delighted in seeing the white-shirted guards returning from a successful hunt, the limp body of a Negro dragging behind a horse. To them Jacobs County was the south as it should have remained, and they kept the secret well.

Mr. Samuel Jacobs, Sr., died in 1892 at the age of eighty, and Sam, Jr., continued building his father's dream empire.

By 1920, fewer than a dozen Negroes who had personal knowledge of the Civil War remained, and in time even they forgot that they had been emancipated. Slavery to them was better than death. They ceased to resist. The guards dwindled away to one sheriff and three deputies, and the white people of Jacobs County were often heard to say, "Our niggers are the freest niggers in the world."

～ *Two*

I T WAS SAID that Granny Jacobs had the best baby-bouncing lap in Jacobsville, and mothers from the most distant parts of the county sooner or later were forced to journey to her shack so their children could have their turn on the lap of love. She did indeed love children, but she never spoiled them, and those who tried to take advantage of her soon found themselves being warmed by her worn slipper. But half the fun of being watched by Granny was the spankings. The slipper was scarcely thicker than a sheet of paper, and once she had punished a child she loved him all the more. She had loved and punished and loved half the white adults of Jacobs County; it was said that if you hadn't been spanked by Granny Jacobs you just hadn't lived.

She hadn't always taken care of other people's children. Back before Jesse was born, and during the first eight years of his life, she took in washing for a living. She was much younger in those days, and although she was even then a great-grandmother, she walked with a quick step and washed with firm hands. As she went about collecting laundry from the various white ladies in the town, she could be heard coming a quarter of a mile away, her voice ringing out in "Go Tell It on the Mountain" or "Rock My Soul in the Bosom of Abraham" or "Swing Low, Sweet Chariot" or any number of the other spirituals and hymns she had known since childhood.

Six days a week she collected, washed, and ironed, and returned the laundry to the rich ladies, to the good ladies, to the kind ladies who sometimes paid her in currency and sometimes in old clothes and sometimes in food, and who sometimes just thought about paying her. On the seventh day, on God's day, her voice was heard with those of the other women of her race in the Mt. Zion Baptist Church.

"A body spends six days workin', and the seventh day is suppose' to be God's day, Jesse," she had told the little boy long before he was old enough to know that sounds were words and words were a means of communication. And God's day to Granny meant being in close proximity to the church from sunup to sundown.

The church was around the corner from the cotton field at the very edge of Mr. Jacobs' plantation, and Mr. Jacobs had promised that he would regularly furnish paint for the building. But time seemed to have little meaning for him, at least in this matter, and the summer before Granny lost Jesse to the world the dried clapboards had been given their first coat of paint in twenty years. From then on, Granny never failed to comment about the church as she approached it on Sunday mornings.

"Lawd, what a beautiful house of God," she always said, bowing her head in reverence.

She and her friends brought their food for lunch and dinner, and cooked on the grounds during the warm weather and in the basement in the winter. The House of God was like nothing else in their world; Preacher Harris made it so exciting with his shouting, singing sermons that Granny felt it was almost sinful for her to enjoy worship so much.

But night would soon come upon them and Granny would walk home, around the cotton field, through the forest, and into her one-room shack, where she would put Jesse to bed on his straw mattress, make a pan of coffee on the little potbelly stove, and look at the pictures in her Bible with the aid of the kerosene lantern and the moonlight streaming through the cracks in the walls, until she fell asleep on the cot.

Monday morning she would be off to take in laundry again, still rejoicing over Sunday, singing at the top of her voice.

Three

THE NEGROES OF Jacobs County were proud people. They were proud not to be white. And contrary to the old tradition that assigns a special place to the first-born male, it was their practice to honor the first-born child of a first-born child regardless of sex, because these were the only children believed to be pure of race. No one remembered how the custom had started, but down the years it had become firmly established, and they continued to celebrate joyously for the increasingly rare first-borns who were genuinely Negro.

To ensure the continued birth of such children was not an easy matter. Often an attractive girl had to be married before she reached puberty, and during the hot summer months, when the white boys and older men from town went out looking for fun, guards had to be stationed at intervals to warn of the approaching danger. By the time the white men reached the girl's house, she would not be there; she and her youthful husband would have hurried off to hide in the woods until the night was over, or until the men's passions had been satisfied by someone else.

Sometimes a sister was noble enough to stay behind and sacrifice herself, knowing the experience would leave her torn and twisting in agony for days. But there were women in Jacobsville who regularly served as substitutes, women like Bessie James and Lula Ferguson, and the other Negroes thanked God for them. Bessie and Lula had a way with white men; they would come out of the shadows and make all kinds of lewd remarks, teasing and arousing and provoking the men into running after them into the woods. If an election had been held among the Negroes to choose the most important ones among them, Bessie James and Lula Ferguson would have won hands down; and although it was suspected that they actually enjoyed their position as substitutes, they were not permitted to work too hard. It was the responsibility of the families of the holy first-borns to provide for them, and often both children and parents went to bed hungry so that Bessie and Lula would have their fill.

Lula's introduction to the white boys came entirely by choice. She had slept with many of the Negro youths, and had no fear of what might happen to her, and one day she walked boldly up to a group of white men who were tugging at a young girl and said, "Why don't y'all leave that little skinny girl alone and get yourself a real woman?"

"Like you?" one of the men said, slapping her on the butt.

"That's right," she said, tossing her dress up, and then she ran laughing into the woods with the men tracking her like hound dogs. She was short and full-breasted; her skin was almost chocolate brown, and she had big wide eyes that could make men happy just to look at them.

Bessie was tall and thin, with long straight legs, a high pointed behind, and small firm breasts. She was not a first-born, but her parents were sure she would be able to marry a good man (perhaps one who was a favorite of Mr. Jacobs) because her smooth olive skin and reddish hair made her particularly attractive in their world—she was almost like a white woman.

It was a bad summer the year Bessie turned twelve, the summer of the floods and the storms. Everyone knew something worse than anything that had ever happened before in Jacobsville was going to happen, and it did.

Bessie, who was already fully grown, had been out walking with young Clay Jenkins, a tall, very dark youth of sixteen with broad shoulders and a full chest. Five white boys passed through the colored section of Jacobsville, storming into shacks and pulling wives and daughters out one by one and forcing them to raise their dresses or take them off there on the street.

At one house a little girl ran outside and said, "Y'all wanna see my pretty legs?" and raised her dress up to her waist. Some of the boys laughed. "Not yet, girl," one of them whined. "Not yet."

At another house they forced a pregnant woman to show

herself to them. "Man oh man, look at that big stomach. Turn around and let us see you shake it, girl."

One of the boys became sickened by the spectacle, and persuaded the others to leave with him. He felt ashamed. Too many people were watching. But when he and his friends came upon Bessie and Clay, there were no outsiders to see them, and they decided they would each of them have Bessie.

As soon as Clay and Bessie saw the boys they ducked into the woods, hoping to escape; but Clay soon realized the only chance Bessie had was for him to stay and fight.

"Run, Bessie!" he shouted. "Run! I'll hol' 'em off." He looked quickly for something to use as a weapon, spotted a fallen branch, broke off the small end, and prepared to defend the honor of his girl.

"Don't worry about this nigger," a boy shouted. "We'll take care of him. You catch her."

One of the boys veered away from Clay and started after Bessie. Clay turned to chase him, caught up with him, and split his skull open with one blow from the club. He turned back in time to see another boy take off after Bessie, but by now the others had caught up with him, and he began swinging away at them. He hit the first one in the face and saw blood go splattering in all directions in the moonlight. The second had gotten behind him and jumped on his back, but Clay threw him over his head and kicked him in the groin and stomach until he stopped groaning. The third boy took off for the road. Clay had chased him for what seemed to be only a few seconds when he saw the lights of town ahead of him and knew what he had done. He had forgotten Bessie now and when the awful realization of what would happen to him flashed through his mind, he broke out in a cold sweat, turned around, and began running as fast as he could in the opposite direction—north.

He had seen lynchings before. He had seen a man castrated. He had seen a man torn apart limb by limb. He had seen men beaten to death with clubs. He had seen white men lash knives to sticks, surround a Negro, and then, bracing the sticks against their chests, cut him until he could stand the pain no longer and threw his full weight against the knives, committing suicide. He had seen men cut so many times that their flesh looked like one huge mass of raw meat. This was one of the white man's more enjoyable games.

He should never have fought. He should have run away the way he was supposed to. He didn't know if the three boys were dead, but it didn't matter. They might just as well be dead because the white men would surely kill him, and he knew they would kill him slowly. He knew he had no right to hit a white man, and so he ran north—north to a world he had heard was better. He ran north to an unknown world of more white people, who were said to be genuinely human.

He didn't know that Bessie had not gotten away, that the second boy had caught her in the woods and that she had fought him until her arms and legs ached and she could fight no more. He didn't know that she had said to the boy, then,

"If y'all be gentle I'll make it good for you, and I'll be your special girl." All Clay knew was that he had to get north so he could stop running.

Clay's action made life unbearable for the other Negroes of Jacobsville. He had killed the three boys, and for months afterward there were lynchings and beatings. Just when the Negroes were certain that things had settled down to what they accepted as normal, someone in town would remember the way the white boys looked when they had been brought into the sheriff's office, and before the night was over several more Negroes would be tortured to death.

The Negroes managed to survive this reign of lynchings as they had survived others in the past, and they sang songs about Clay. He was their hero, and they didn't believe what the white men told them, that he had been caught and lynched on the spot. They knew he had escaped the hounds. They knew there wasn't a dog in the county that could catch Clay. They knew he would run until he died rather than be caught. They had no way of knowing positively that Clay had made it to the north, but they believed he must have.

"After all," one of the old men said, "if they had done caught that boy they sho 'nuf woulda done brought him back here so's we could see what they done to him."

No, they weren't positive, but they believed Clay had escaped—running all the way to Chicago.

It was on the night of Clay's escape that Bessie got down on her knees and begged God to forgive her for what she was going to do. "But I just can't let it happen no mo', Lawd," she said. "Long as I live, ifen that's all they wants, I'll see to it that nobody else gets kilt." And she assumed her role as a substitute, as a charmer of white men and boys, to save the first-borns so that her people could have something to be proud of.

Bessie and Lula might have been considered evil women except for the fact that they sat in the first pew in the church and never once missed a Sunday.

This kind of devotion to the first-borns enabled Granny Jacobs, herself a first-born, to save her granddaughter for Jesse Black.

Granny would much rather they had been able to get married, but by the time Bertha reached puberty the white people were more determined than ever to stop the tradition. They had heard, from a Negro trying to win favor among them, that the man who got this last pure black woman would have pleasures he would remember for a lifetime. This gave them even more reason to have a black woman: they delighted in breaking the chain of first-borns, and it had gotten so that many Jacobsville Negroes were light enough to pass for white.

Some of the old women came to Granny, the summer Bertha's breasts became so noticeable, and told her they thought it best to get her away for a while. They feared the violence that might result if the white men caught her.

Bertha was the last first-born, all the others having given birth to half-white children long before, and the Negroes might fight rather than let her fall into the lustful hands of a white man. The old women entered into the selection of a suitable mate for her, as was their custom, but this time the privilege was taken away from them. Bertha had already chosen Jesse Black, the young son of Mr. Jacobs' field manager.

Jesse was eighteen years old and as big and as black and as fine-looking a young man as anybody in Jacobs County had ever seen. All of the women admired him—the white women as well as the Negroes—but Jesse had decided, long before Bertha reached maturity, that she would be his mate. So when he knew her future was being planned, he took her with him and broke in on the meeting of the old women.

"Bertha and me decided we gonna get married," Jesse announced.

The women were shocked.

Before they could offer an argument, he continued, "I done saved myself for this here girl and y'all knows as well as the Lawd that I sho didn't have to. I saved myself for her and for our baby and there ain't no other man in the whole of Jacobs County, colored or white, can say that. Besides, she wants me and I wants her."

"I do, Granny," Bertha said softly, then turning away from Jesse's eyes, "I wants him, too."

Granny Jacobs smiled. "Yes, child," she said. "Now y'all step out and let us finish."

The two young people left the shack and waited outside under a tree.

At first the women were angry that Jesse and Bertha had

defied them, but after a few moments' discussion, they conceded that Jesse looked to be as pure as a first-born and since the only requirement for the mate of a first-born was that he look one-hundred-per-cent Negro, Jesse was as sound a choice as they could make. Besides, there was good blood in his veins and had been as far back as they could trace it, and Bertha's child by him should be a truly special first-born because this would be the first time, as far as they knew, that a girl had ever married the man she wanted.

It was decided. Jesse and Bertha would be man and wife and give the people of Jacobs County another first-born child.

There was no time to waste. The women gathered enough food to sustain the couple for a week, left it with Granny, and departed to keep watch for white men.

Granny was crying as she walked into the woods with Jesse and Bertha. She put her arms around them and said, "In my eyes and in the eyes of the Lawd y'all's now married folk." She wiped the tears away from her eyes. "Jesse," she said, "don't y'all come outta them hills 'til summer's over. And I prays to the Lawd Bertha's bearin' a child when you does."

"Yes, ma'am," Jesse said. He threw the three sacks of food over his shoulder and led his young companion deeper into the woods.

They lived in the hills all summer. Jesse came down at night and stole food from some of the farmers; during the day, he hunted small animals. He and Bertha were very much in love, and it was the most beautiful honeymoon a Jacobsville couple had ever had.

That September, when the weather cooled off and the white men had forgotten about Bertha, she and Jesse came back. It was a joyous day for the Negroes of Jacobsville, and there was dancing and drinking and barbecuing, because Bertha was three months pregnant and the chain had not been broken. Granny Jacobs was so happy that every time she looked at Bertha she broke into tears of joy. And Jesse was proud, proud to have been picked as the maker of a first-born child.

Bertha's pregnancy was not an easy one. Toward the end of it there were many bad nights, when she became feverish; and she had to be cared for twenty-four hours a day. Jesse became irritable, and on one occasion, when he was working in the fields, he spoke back to Mr. Jacobs himself. Mr. Jacobs over-looked this breach of conduct because he knew about Jesse and Bertha and, although he couldn't show how he felt, he admired them. When little Jesse was born, Mr. Jacobs brought enough clothing to last for years.

Bertha died two months after the baby was born, just as her mother had, and on the way back from the funeral Jesse refused to move for the deputy sheriff.

"Nigger," the deputy said. "Did you hear me tell you to move?"

Jesse didn't answer.

"Don't you hear me, nigger? I'll make you hear me." He

slipped his baton out of the ring, raised his arm, and started swinging down with all his might. Jesse caught his arm and snapped his wrist with a loud crack. The deputy's eyes bulged with shock and disbelief, and he screamed in pain. Jesse raised the club and came down on his skull with powerful, rapid strokes. The deputy fell to the ground dead. Jesse would have to leave Jacobsville. He would have to run away, and although he was willing to take the baby, Granny Jacobs wouldn't hear of it.

"This here baby's the last real first-born," she told him. "And I ain't about to let you kill him out there. Ifen y'all gets away and gets up there to Chicago, make one of them smart colored folks write Preacher Harris, 'cause he's always gettin' letters anyway, and just tell him y'all's all right, and when the boy's old enough I'll get him up to you. I don't know how, but I'll get him there somehow."

Jesse left with his closest friend, K.C., heading north. The people hid the deputy's body, and it was not discovered for three days, more than enough time for K.C. and Jesse to get out of Mississippi. Two months later Preacher Harris received a post card with a picture of many tall buildings and a wide street called Michigan Avenue. On the back of the card was written the word "Hebbin," and they knew K.C. and Jesse had made it to freedom.

Four

GRANNY RAISED little Jesse as if he were a white boy—a prince who would someday have to leave her to go up north. He was an exceptional child in any case, and it was her wish that he should know more than the other Negro children had known.

By the time he was five he had learned all the hymns they sang in church, and he had a beautiful soprano voice. When he was six Mr. Jacobs allowed him to accompany his youngest son to school, and at seven he could read and write as well as the average ten-year-old. Mr. Jacobs had granted Granny the use of his piano when he heard that the boy was musically inclined, and at the age of eight Little Jesse could play better than Mr. Jacobs himself.

When Mr. Jacobs was giving a party at the big house and wanted to impress his friends, he would send for Jesse, and Granny would dress him in the suit Mr. Jacobs had brought back from Jackson, and the little boy would play the piano from five o'clock in the afternoon until nine or ten at night.

He loved to play the piano but he hated to play for Mr. Jacobs' friends, and one day when Mr. Jacobs sent for him, Jesse refused to go. It was then that Granny realized how much like his father the boy was. He began talking back to white people that year, and if it hadn't been for Mr. Jacobs standing guardian over him, the sheriff would have beaten the little boy. Because Mr. Jacobs felt the way he did about Jesse, all the sheriff could do was talk about him and say that when the old man died he would get him, he would break him before he got to be a man.

Granny heard the talk that had been circulating among white people in front of their Negro help and she decided it was time for Jesse to join his father in Chicago. She didn't know where Big Jesse lived, but she knew Negroes must have a way of finding each other and she was sure the people who took the boy to Chicago would be able to find Big Jesse or K.C.

She had heard of a Negro family, over in neighboring Jackson County, that was preparing to go north. The only possible way for her to get Jesse to them was to take him herself, through the woods and the Negro section of the town of Minnott, praying to God that she could find them and persuade them to take Jesse, and return to Jacobsville without having been seen by any whites. But she knew the trip would take at least three days; the white ladies would want their laundry done, and would miss her if she were gone that long. To compound her problems, she would have to travel at night, and that would make the journey twice as slow. If they caught her they'd surely do to her what they did to the other Negroes who tried to leave; they'd shoot her and the boy down and dig a hole and cover them over and forget all about it without telling Mr. Jacobs or anyone else.

That's what they'd do, Granny thought. They'd just kill me quick as battin' an eye—and my Little Jesse, too.

But she had to try it, because Mr. Jacobs wouldn't live forever, and even he couldn't protect Jesse after he grew up and left the immunity of childhood to become just another Negro hand to work in the fields. No, she had to try it, because the Black Prince was the last of the first-borns and she knew he would never reach maturity in Jacobsville.

The old women got together again and worked out a plan. Granny Jacobs was going to be gone six days, so they would take in the washing for her while she was gone and Granny Jones would stay in her house and pretend to be ill and they would say that Granny Jacobs was caring for Granny Jones. But what would they do if one of the white people decided to visit Granny Jones? Well, they'd have to cross that bridge when they came to it. No, they would say that Granny Jacobs wasn't there because she had gone out to get some food or water or something. It would work. Of course it would work.

It would work because not even the sheriff would suspect that Granny might try to sneak out of Jacobsville. But he would be angry if he ever found out, because more than anything else he wanted to teach Jesse some manners and break him once and for all.

They'd have to get a box made and put a few bricks in it, and when Granny came back they'd hold a funeral and bury the box just as if Little Jesse were in it. That was the only way they could keep the sheriff from finding out the truth about Little Jesse's disappearance. But Mr. Jacobs would be so hurt, they thought. Oh, Lawd, he would be so hurt, and his little son, little Clyde, would be hurt to lose his playmate.

"It don't matter none," Granny said. "Our Black Prince has gotta have a chance to grow up like a man."

The old women nodded their heads in agreement and the plan went into operation.

It was decided that Granny would leave Thursday night, two hours after the sun went down, when it was good and black outside.

"Besides," Aunt Agnes said, "that way you sho to have three days 'fo they start worryin' 'bout you, 'cause white folks ain't got their senses 'bout 'em on the weekends. All they ever cares 'bout is sittin' around restin' up for the day after Sunday while we works just as hard as ever Friday and Saturday and some- times even Sunday."

Yes, Granny thought, she's sho 'nuf right 'bout that. Let's see—Thursday, Friday, Saturday, Sunday, Monday, Tuesday,

Wednesday? Is that the day I be back? I sho pray to the Lawd I will.

The old women prepared food enough for Granny and Jesse, and they put it in two sacks. Jesse was a strong little boy and he had to carry his own food if Granny was to have enough energy to get there, even though she protested that she should carry both sacks.

Thursday night, just before the sun went down, Uncle Otis knocked on the door, and when Granny opened it he was standing there dressed in his Sunday hat with a shotgun resting on his shoulder. He was like a picture of a soldier Granny had seen in a magazine, back in the times before Mrs. Jacobs discovered she had been looking at the pictures and warned her that she mustn't ever do that again, because those magazines were not for her; if the sheriff ever heard of it he'd have her whipped until she almost turned white. And that would be some whippin', Granny thought at that time. That would sho 'nuf be some whippin'.

"Just where you think you goin', Otis?"

"With you. You and that boy can't never make it there 'cause you don't even know which way the sun comes up in the mornin'."

Otis had always spoken gruffly to Granny. He was sixty-five years old now, three years older than she was, old enough to draw old-age assistance if Mr. Barnes had ever filed for him. He was surely old enough to stop working, and Mr. Barnes had taken him out of the cotton field and put him back in the barn where he could count the bales as they were made up. Mr. Barnes was good to his colored folks that way.

Otis wasn't as handsome as he used to be years before, back when Granny had allowed herself to think that they might get married because her husband had been dead for ten years then and Otis' wife for three. He had been tall and lean, with long firm muscles, and he walked with a long proud stride. Granny used to look at him in those days and sigh. She was sure he had it in mind to propose to her eventually; for a while he used to stop by the house almost every week just to ask how she was feeling and how the washing was going, and hundreds of other questions that men don't ask unless they're thinking about courting.

But he never did ask, Granny thought now, as she looked at the old man, his shoulders stooped and his bald head shining in the light from the house and hundreds of white stubs sticking out of his face. He's still a handsome man to me, but he just never did get around to askin'. But that's what he gets for workin' around that Mr. Barnes for so long. Huh, Mr. Barnes didn't even get around to marryin' a white woman until he was almost fifty, and after that black woman done had all them children for him, too. Sho do work slow, some of these white folks. And these white folks' colored folks work just as slow. Maybe nex' year . . .

"Suppose you come on a bear or a cat or some other critters? You wouldn't even know which way to run. Besides, you can't carry all that food noways. I got mines out here," he said, pointing down next to the door. "Look at you, you ain't much bigger than a peck. How you gonna carry them bags?"

Granny blushed. She was sixty-two and as brown as chocolate, but her face just opened up and turned reddish all over. Ain't he sweet now, she said to herself.

"Well, don't stand out there and let all the white folks passin' by know what we's gonna do. Step inside while I gets my things fixed."

Otis hesitated for a second, as he had for the past twenty years, and then stepped over the threshold.

They left that night. Jesse had slept all day and was wide awake and very alert during the hike through the woods. He took a knife Mr. Jacobs had given him and trimmed two branches to make walking sticks for Granny and Otis; then he made one for himself. He had been through the woods many times as a companion for Clyde when Mr. Jacobs had taken them hunting. Indeed, he was the only Negro in Jacobs County who had ever been almost to the county line with a white man. As the sun started to come up he told them they were approaching the swamp, and it would be necessary for them to head north a few miles to find dry land that would lead them around it.

"How far is it 'til we gets to some more woods, boy?" Otis asked.

"Oh, 'bout four miles, Mr. Jacobs used to always say."

"Reckon we can get there 'fo the sun gets too high?"

"Never took us no too long. Mr. Jacobs got a house back in

the hills down there. We could use that. He ain't gonna do no huntin' this week. Next week me and Clyde was to go."

Granny was proud of her great-grandson. He never disappointed her. That boy knows more about things right now than I ever will if I live to be a hundred, she thought. The Black Prince of Jacobsville. That's what he is, all right. He's our Prince, and some day he'll come back and maybe . . . Well, now, don't get your hopes up none. Besides, you ain't even prayed for it yet and already you plannin' and plannin' just like you knew it was gonna happen. That's what I say about you, Granny Jacobs, sometimes you just plans and plans things 'til you almost makes them happen even without them happenin'. White folks plans things 'cause they can. But you don't have to plan nothin' because it don't matter none what you plan. If things is to happen they happen and there ain't nothin' you or nobody else can do about them 'cep the Lawd, and He makes them happen just like he wants them to, so there.

They reached the cabin just as the sun broke over the hills. They stood on the porch, not wanting to violate a law they had respected for so long. Neither Granny nor Otis quite dared to turn the knob and open the door. Jesse stood between them for a full minute, waiting, before he sensed the fear that was in their eyes, stepped boldly forward, turned the knob, and kicked the door open the way he had seen Mr. Jacobs do. He walked to the big rocking chair next to the fireplace, sat down, and began rocking as fast as he could.

"It's okay, Granny," he called out. "Mr. Jacobs don't mind none if I'm here with you."

The old friends smiled at each other and walked wearily into the cottage.

Granny sliced some bread and made salt pork sandwiches. Otis went out to the well, and Jesse accompanied him, pointing out things he and Clyde had discovered when they had gone exploring around the cottage.

"That boy sure knows a lot," Otis whispered to Granny as she cleared the crumbs from the table. "That's just why the sheriff hates him so. He's too dang smart for him. First thing you know, by the time he growed up he'd have the folks makin' him sheriff."

Granny laughed, because she knew even the Black Prince could never be anything other than a field hand in Jacobs County. Lawd, Lawd, she thought, it just ain't right for me to have to let him go so soon, but if that's the way you wants it, Lawd, that's the way it's gotta be.

She tucked Jesse into a big bed upstairs in one of the bedrooms and kissed him good night, and then she recited a verse from the Bible, one of the many she had heard Preacher Harris say.

"Granny," Jesse said, just before he fell asleep.

"Yes, son."

"Will you tell Clyde how much fun we had when you get back? We never had this much fun with Mr. Jacobs. Clyde would like . . ."

She kissed him again and went downstairs, where she fell asleep in the rocking chair. Otis put two blankets on the floor and slept with his back against the door.

Five

THE JOURNEY didn't take nearly as long as they had expected. The next night, after they had been traveling only a few hours, they came to the outskirts of a town. They were not sure that it was Minnott, nor were they sure the colored section would be where they had been told it was. For all they knew, they might still be in Jacobs County. But they had been told by some of the old people when they were younger that Jacobs County was not much larger than the town of Jacobsville and that Minnott was the first town to the north. They'd have to believe what their minds told them they had heard. Yes, they must be out of Jacobs County, but they would still have to be careful. The white people of Mississippi were proud of Jacobs County for stopping the clock and preserving the old way of life. They would think nothing of rounding up Granny and Otis and Jesse, putting them in a car, and driving them right back where they came from—right back to the sheriff.

They crossed somebody's property line and Otis and Jesse helped Granny over the fence. They heard hounds bark far away near the big house, hurried across a field, and walked on for what seemed to be hours before they reached a small group of houses.

"Reckon that's it, Granny?" Otis asked quietly.

Granny stood sniffing at the wind, with Jesse looking up at her, head cocked, mouth open, trying to discern what she was doing. "No," she said finally. "Let's keep on agoin'."

"How you know that ain't it?" Otis asked.

"Garbage," she said, stepping over a mound of dirt.

"Garbage? You all right, Bertha?"

Granny felt warm inside. He called me by my name, she thought. He ain't done that but one other time that I can remember. I declare, he sho must be worried for me.

"Sho I'm sho," she said confidently. "Who you know don't burn their own garbage?"

Otis thought for a minute. It was difficult for him to think because he was tired and his legs ached and his back ached and his neck ached from turning around every fifty yards to see if they were being followed. Even his mind was tired, so tired that if he didn't get a chance to sit down soon he felt his head would split open. But then it dawned on him and he said, "Po' white folks?"

"That's right. Po' white folks the only ones that can't get colored folks to burn their garbage and lets it pile up 'til it smells as bad as the hounds."

They continued due north until they came on more shacks, rows and rows of them, some with roads that led right up beside them, some so large they must have four and five rooms each. Granny was really frightened now, and stopped to muster enough courage to proceed to one of the houses.

It's just gotta be the colored section, she thought. The colored section's always the biggest. But suppose this ain't it and these is really white folks and the colored section is somewheres else? Oh, Lawd, help us.

"Come on, Jesse," she said, taking the little boy by the hand. They walked a block in back of the houses, and then turned through one of the driveways that led out into a dirt road and walked along the road staring in amazement at the houses that lined it on both sides.

"I don't know," Otis said. "I ain't never seed no colored folks with houses like this."

Granny thought: Well, now, he just might—no, it's colored folks. I can tell.

She led Jesse to a small shack, stopped at the door, and paused for a few seconds, contemplating the many possible consequences of her next move. In the end she sighed and knocked gently. She thought: If there's colored folks there they'll hear that. White folks sleep so sound they can't hear a thunderstorm, but colored folks can hear an owl a half-mile away.

Before long there was the sound of someone moving about in the house, slowly approaching the door. Then the door opened, quickly, so fast that it seemed to Granny to be closed one second and wide open the next, and standing framed in the doorway was a Negro as big as Big Jesse.

"Who is it?" he growled.

"Don't you raise your voice to me none, boy," Granny snapped.

"Who y'all?" the man said, lowering his voice.

"That's better. I'm Granny Jacobs and this here is Otis and this here is Jesse Jacobs, Little Jesse the first-born, the Black Prince. Now where's them folks that's headin' for Chicago live at?"

The man's mouth dropped open and he stood mute, staring at Jesse and Granny with eyes almost as big as Jesse's head.

"I'm Jesse Jacobs," the little boy said, extending his hand as he had seen the white people do so often.

The man took his hand with two fingers and a thumb. "I'm pleased to meet you, boy—ah, sir—ah, Mr. Jacobs," he said and resumed staring.

"Don't stand there all night, boy," Granny said. "We gotta get done with our business and get back to Jacobsville before daybreak."

"Yes, ma'am." The man ducked behind the door and returned in a moment, buckling his belt. "It's right over there," he said, pointing across the street to one of the larger houses. "It's young Robert Lee Brown and his new wife." He led them to the house and knocked heavily on the door.

"Now don't knock the door down, boy," Granny said.

"No, ma'am. I sho won't."

A woman opened the door.

"Let us in," the man said softly. "These folks from Jacobsville with . . ." He swallowed. "With the boy—with the Prince."

"Hurry," the woman said, waving them through the door. Once they were inside she closed the door and they could hear her moving about. She struck a match and lit a lamp, which she held high above her head while she stared in disbelief, as the man had done.

"Robert! Robert, Junior! Ruth Ellen! Y'all come down here. Hurry, Robert. I can't believe it. I just can't believe it."

Two men and a young woman came down the stairs. The men were carrying shotguns and the woman looked very frightened.

"What is it, honey?" the older man said.

She pointed to Granny. "They're from Jacobsville. They're from Jacobsville and that's the boy."

"I'm Granny Jacobs and this here is Otis and this here is Jesse, he's the last of the first-borns."

Jesse stepped forward to greet them.

The older gentleman said, "I'm Robert Brown."

"Okay. Pleased to meet you," Jesse said, extending his hand.

The man shook hands and bowed slightly. "This is my wife, Clare Brown."

Jesse shook her hand and she too bowed.

"And this is my son, Robert Lee, Junior. He's the one's goin' to Chicago."

Robert bowed and smiled as the little boy shook his hand. "And this is Robert's wife, Ruth Ellen."

Ruth curtsied, ignored Jesse's hand, and hugged him.

Granny smiled. These is good people, she thought. He'll be all right with these people. Thank you, Lawd. Thank you, Jesus.

"Well, don't just stand there," Mrs. Brown said. "Get some chairs for these people. They must be tired and hungry. Ruth Ellen, come with me and we'll fix some food." She turned and walked to the kitchen. "I just can't believe it," she said to Ruth Ellen.

The men placed chairs around the table and lit another lamp.

Jesse walked into the kitchen and looked at the big stove; it was almost as big as the one Mr. Jacobs had at the cottage.

Granny sat down. "Thank the Lawd," she said out loud. "Thank the Lawd for deliverin' us to such good folks." She turned to the man behind her. "Thank you for showin' us the way. But I don't believe we never did find out your name."

"LeRoy, ma'am. LeRoy Davis, and if I live to be a thousand years old I don't reckon I'll never ever be nowheres near as happy as I am right now to see you and that there boy."

"I hear tell," Granny said, turning back to Mr. Brown, "that white folks pay colored folks over here to help them get us colored folks back to Jacobs County."

"I'm sorry to say that's right, Granny," Mr. Brown said. "Most of us try to help, but there's always them few."

"I sho hope that don't happen to my boy."

"Don't you worry none, Granny," LeRoy said. "The bus depot's no more than about twenty miles from here, and when Robert and Ruth Ellen leaves I'm gonna be right there, and if we so much as meets anybody that looks at us too long—" he held his hands up and jerked them quickly as if he were snapping a twig—"that's what they'll get."

Granny sat back in the chair and relaxed for the first time in days. "So many good folks," she said.

"But tell me," the senior Mr. Brown said. "I don't understand something. White folks around here been sayin' for years that there wasn't no mo' first-borns left in Jacobs County."

"There ain't. Not now there ain't. This here boy's the last one. Lawd, we used to have a whole lotta first-borns, but the white men heard about it, and next thing we knew we had so many colored folks turnin' up white we couldn't keep track of 'em. And so after a while the last one left was my daughter. Only way we saved her was by tellin' the white folks there wasn't no mo'. And then my granddaughter was born and now him. He's my great-grandson," she said proudly. "And his pappy left outta Jacobs County with his best friend the same year the boy was born. I know he got up to Chicago 'cause he sent a letter to the preacher sayin' he was there."

"There was two men," the senior Mr. Brown said, "oh, a long time ago, and they came through here one night runnin' as fast as race horses. The next mornin' some Uncle Tom Negro went to the sheriff and told him, and the sheriff took off after them, but he couldn't catch them. No, suh, them boys could smell freedom, and there just wasn't no catchin' up with them, not them two."

"That's his pappy, all right," Granny said, smiling broadly. "He just like him. Why, he talks back to white folks and can sing like someone you ain't never heard before and read and write already. He can even play that piano, and bettern Mr. Jacobs, too. We don't mind stayin' behind—we old—but if he stays the sheriff'll try to break him, and he can't be broke 'cause he was born to be free and we just know they'll sho have to kill him."

"Ruth Ellen and me was going to leave for Chicago next week, but now I see we'll have to leave tomorrow. We'll take him with us, Granny, and we'll love him just like he was one of our own."

"Thank you, son. I didn't know if y'all folks would do that, but the good Lawd told me to come on and see. I heard tell that somebody here was agoin' north, but I didn't know when or who or nothin'. Just done what I felt was right by the boy."

"How'd you find out?" LeRoy Davis asked.

"Well, now," Otis said, "you know how white folks always talkin' about their colored folks and stuff. Well, one night Mr. Barnes—that's the man I works for—was talkin' to some man from over here and the man from over here said the son of his best worker was leavin' for the north and he wished it was like Jacobs County so's he could stop him and make him stay the way they do us, but he couldn't. Mr. Barnes said he oughta do it like they do over in Jacobs County, and the man said he sure wished he could. I must of heard that last week or so, and when I finds out about it I tells somebody else, and the next thing I knows Granny's makin' plans to come here so's Jesse could join his father up in God's country."

"I wish I could stay and help you folks over there," Robert said. "It don't seem right that somebody can't help out. It ain't much better here, but at least we can get out and go somewhere else, if we can ever make enough money for the bus fare. And if it wasn't for my folks, Ruth Ellen and me wouldn't be able to leave here. When I get up north I'm gonna tell somebody about Jacobs County and maybe then—"

"Better not do that, son," Mr. Brown said. "Them folks got a right to live, too, and you can't never tell what the white folks might do if they found out that somebody knew about things over there."

"Well they sure can't kill all of them."

"They're like animals, son. You know that. You can't tell what they might do. I remember when I was a boy, I heard tell of stories where they killed so many Negroes over there that the rain washed the blood down into the lake and the whole lake turned red from it."

Granny rocked back and forth in the chair and said softly, almost to herself, "Yes, Lawd, they done killed some good folks, so many good folks."

Mrs. Brown handed Granny and Otis a cup of coffee. Granny took the cup, bowed her head, and said, "Thank you now, ma'am." She reached into her bosom and brought out a tobacco sack. She fingered it gently for a moment and then handed it to the young Mr. Brown. "That ain't much, I guess, but it's all I got now. I reckon five dollars ought to pay for some of his passage. When you find Big Jesse he'll pay you the rest."

"Yes, ma'am. But suppose I don't find him?"

Granny smiled. "You'll find him, son. All you gotta do is let them people up in Chicago know you got the last of the first-borns with you and you won't even have to look for him. He find you. He's a proud man and he's gonna want to raise his own son and bring him up so's he can help his people." She pointed to the boy, who was sitting at the kitchen table eating a piece of corn bread. "Ain't nobody can save us but that boy, and somehow he'll do it. I don't know how, but I know he will, and I'm gonna sit right over in Jacobsville 'til he does."

She got to her feet. "Y'all don't fix nothin' for us, if you please. We can't stay. It's best we gets back. We don't want them to miss us. Jesse, come say good-by to yo' Granny."

Jesse dropped the corn bread, ran to his great-grandmother, and threw his arms around her.

She got down on her knees with the help of Otis and held him close to her for a full minute.

"Jesse, boy," she said in a choking voice. "Now you know what you and me talked about, don't you?"

"Yes, Granny."

"Well, now, son, these are the folks that's takin' you to yo' pappy and I wants you to be a good boy for them. And don't tell nobody, never, that you from Jacobsville. You understand, boy?"

"Yes, Granny. I won't tell. I won't tell. Never."

"I know you won't, boy."

"Granny?"

"Yes, son."

"You said we wasn't gonna cry."

"I know, son, but I can't help it."

"I want to cry now, too, Granny," he said, rubbing his nose with the back of his hand.

"No, no, son. You can't cry now. You a Prince, but I'm just yo' old Granny. I ain't nothin', so I can cry. But you show Granny how strong you are, and maybe after Granny leaves, you can cry just a little bit and then you'll be all right."

"Yes, ma'am."

"Come on, Otis. Let's leave these good folks so's they can get back to bed."

"We'll take good care of him," Ruth Ellen said, putting her arm around Jesse.

"Thank you kindly," Granny said. "Y'all's good folks."

The senior Mr. Brown opened the door and Granny and Otis stepped into the night.

"Thank you, Lawd," they heard her say as she and Otis disappeared into the darkness.

Six

THE FUNERAL PROCESSION was the longest and saddest
Jacobsville had ever seen. It seemed to the townspeople
that the Negro women had never cried quite so much as they
did for the little boy. They had not cried so much when the
old preacher died, and even some of the white people were
almost moved to tears.

As the procession passed in back of the white section of
town, the sheriff came out to look at the mourners.

"Dammit," he said, "I sure wanted to get my hands on that
boy, and he had to go and die."

After Preacher Harris had said a few words over the box,
it was lowered into the ground, but just as the gravediggers
started shoveling dirt into the grave, Mr. Jacobs pulled up in
his car and shouted to them to stop. The gravediggers looked
at each other, terrified, and Granny's heart felt as if it was
going to give out.

"Oh Lawd," she said softly. "Oh Lawd, please don't let him find out."

"Pull that damn box up," Mr. Jacobs said.

The men didn't move.

"I said pull it up."

"Yes, suh." The two men jumped into the grave, handed the little box up, and backed away. Mr. Jacobs took a hammer from the back pocket of his trousers and pried the lid open. He looked inside.

A woman in the crowd screamed and fainted. Preacher Harris grew weak, and supported himself on one of the gravediggers.

Otis moved over to Granny as if to protect her from Mr. Jacobs. "I'm sorry, Bertha," he said. "It almost worked."

"It don't matter none now," Granny whispered. "It don't matter none now at all, 'cause he's all the way to the north. Ain't nothin' they can do to him and we so old it don't matter none what they do to us. I sho am sorry for the rest of these folks, though."

Mr. Jacobs lowered the lid, hammered it back in place, turned to Preacher Harris, and said in a loud voice, "Okay, Uncle Harris. But next time you have a funeral, you make damn sure you come to me first. I'm the coroner in this county and I have to say if people are dead before they can be buried."

"Yes, suh, Mr. Jacobs. Yes, suh," Preacher Harris said happily. "Hymn number 225: 'Jesus Is the Light of the World.'"

He began singing and the people joined in. They sang so loud they could be heard for three miles downwind.

Mr. Jacobs walked to Granny, put his arm around her, and said, "I expect you better give up washing now, Aunt Bertha. Besides, you're too old for that. I think maybe you better take care of my son Clyde. Maybe you can make him a man like you did your boy."

Granny nodded, and her voice rang out above all the others: "Jesus is the Light, He's the Light of the world. . . ."

A few years after that the white people stopped calling her Aunt Bertha and referred to her as Granny Jacobs, just like the Negroes. She raised many of the white children in Jacobsville, and when the war started and the white boys went away to fight, they stopped by to say good-by to Granny and asked her to pray for them.

Almost everyone in town grew to respect her, as much as they could ever respect a Negro, because of the way she was with their children. She did not act out of fear, but out of a genuine love for them, and the white people knew it. Before long it was said among them that Granny Jacobs had made some kind of bargain with God, and part of it was that she would devote the rest of her life to helping other people's children.

Part Two

Seven

OVER THE NEXT twenty-five years, Jesse communicated with Granny through Preacher Harris. This was possible only because the postal clerks had grown used to the idea of the preacher's receiving mail, and in time became lax in their inspection of it. They knew from past experience that it always dealt with religious matters, but they still had to go through the mechanics of inspection at least once a year. So in January they would open the first two letters addressed to him, and year after year there would be nothing but printed matter pertaining to the Baptist Church.

Sometimes the sheriff would warn him not to abuse the privileges he had been granted: "Now I told you I don't mind them letters, but if I catch you gettin' anything besides church books, I'll print 'em all over your black hide. You understand that, boy?"

And Preacher Harris would bow and reply, "Yes, suh, Mr. Sheriff. Yes, suh, but I didn't ask them for nothin' wrong. I just wrote for books for the children in Sunday school. That's all, Mr. Sheriff."

"You ain't tryin' to teach them little pickaninnies to read, are you?"

"No, suh, Mr. Sheriff. No more than the word of the Lawd. Just the word of God and that's all."

"That's all right, then, boy. As long as you're teachin' them how to behave and that's all, that's all right. But I don't want them readin' nothin' else but church books. You can't teach them to read noways. Ain't one out of a thousand niggers can read. Just don't let me hear about nothin' else but this shit comin' to you. That's all."

"Yes, suh, Sheriff. Yes, suh, Mr. Sheriff."

One day a letter came from Jesse that sent Preacher Harris jumping up and down like one of the children at the annual church picnic. He was so excited he broke out of the church and ran halfway to Granny's shack before he realized he still had the letter in his hand. He was in luck; there were no white people around. He stopped in his tracks, bent down on one knee, and removed his shoe; pretending to be searching for a pebble, he slipped the letter inside the shoe, which he took great pains to lace tightly before he continued on his way.

Inside Granny's little house he sat at the table and whispered the contents of the letter to her.

"He's writ a book, Granny. He's writ a book 'bout Jacobsville, and it's gonna be printed soon, and he's to be in a magazine that colored folks got in Chicago. He says they took a lot of pictures of him and his wife and his baby, and you be able to see it if we can get a copy of the magazine."

Granny was pleased that Jesse had had a book published, but not being able to read she was not nearly as excited as she became when Preacher Harris read: "So two months from now *Ebony* will print the story they did on me and you'll be able to see me and my wife and your great-great-grandson, if I can smuggle a copy in to you. I'll do it, Granny, if I have to send a page at a time."

My boy in a picture magazine made by colored folks, she thought. Holy Jesus, I want to see that.

"Preacher Harris," she said, "how I go 'bout seein' one of them books?"

Preacher Harris thought for a long time; he thought for what seemed as long a time as it took him to come out of one of those trances he would go into when he was preaching so well that the sisters fainted from excitement. Finally he said, "Well, I reckon the best way is for you to do what they call subscribe to the magazine. If they catch me this time, Granny, I'm dead for sho. But I don't figure as I'd ever live as long as you noways, so it don't make no nevermind."

Now Preacher Harris was no real ordained preacher. Mr. Jacobs had picked him out of the fields one day, after the old preacher had been dead for a while, because he sensed among the Negroes a need for a new spiritual leader; he had him taught to read and write, and gave him a black suit and white shirt, and paraded him around before the other white people, showing him off as "the new nigger preacher who learned to read and write in the same year and who can shout and pant just as good as any nigger preacher in Mississippi or anywhere else."

Preacher Harris was a tall man, and over the years he filled out to match the image that was expected of him. In time he was reading the Bible as if he had attended school and had been reading it all his life; soon, with a little help from within and without, he became a man of God. His only sin was in knowing about Little Jesse and allowing the correspondence to go on through him.

He had to be very careful, because of course he had no way of knowing when one of the white men in the post office would open a letter and read it. He had decided that two letters a year was all he could send to Jesse and he cautioned Jesse not to write more often than that himself. As a result of this careful planning, the deception had worked for twenty-five years. Mr. Jacobs died without ever having discovered that Preacher Harris had sinned against him.

After he had decided to subscribe to the magazine for Granny, Preacher Harris took five dollars from the church treasury, mumbled a quick prayer to God, and slipped the money into an envelope addressed to Ebony Magazine, Chicago, Illinois, and then placed it in another envelope addressed to The Baptist Periodical, just as he always did with his letters to Jesse. He and Granny knelt in church for a full twenty minutes in prayer and then they got up and walked into town to mail the subscription.

The first copy of the magazine, a back issue, came two weeks later, and, as it happened, was opened by the postmaster himself. He and the other white men in the post office were amazed to see a magazine about Negroes, and he sent for the sheriff immediately. He meant to keep all knowledge of it from the Negro workers in the post office, who had been taught to read names and addresses so they could sort mail. But he became so excited when the sheriff arrived that he let the news slip, right in front of everybody:

"Sheriff, it's all about niggers—northern niggers with big houses and cars. It ain't nothin' but niggers, Sheriff. Not even none of them damn northern Jews. Just niggers. And they even live bettern us!"

The Negroes continued sorting mail as if they had heard nothing.

The sheriff took the postmaster's arm, flung him out the door, and whispered to him angrily: "You out of your mind. Them niggers heard every word you said."

"I couldn't help it. When I saw you it just blurted out. Here it is. See for yourself."

The sheriff flipped the pages of the magazine quickly, stopped to smile at the picture of a woman modeling a bathing suit, and went on flipping the pages more slowly. By the time he finished he was breathing heavily, as if he had just run a great distance. He stood slapping the magazine in the palm of his hand, red-faced and snorting.

"It's a lie," he said. "It's a goddamn lie. Ain't no niggers nowhere ever lived bettern me. Who the fuck was supposed to get this thing?"

"It's right on there," the postmaster said. "Right there. It says: 'Mrs. Bertha Jacobs, Jacobsville, Mississippi.' That's who it's for, old Granny Jacobs."

"Come on," the sheriff said, pushing him into the squad car. "I'll break that old bitch's neck."

The car skidded to a halt in front of Granny's house, throwing up a cloud of dust. Granny was sitting on the stoop, rocking a white baby in her arms and singing softly.

"Mornin', Sheriff. Mornin', Mr. Howard," she said.

The sheriff jumped from the car, hurried to Granny, and threw the magazine on the ground at her feet.

"Granny!" he shouted. "What do you know about this?"

Granny's eyes sparkled as she saw the picture of the handsome, dark-brown-skinned Negro with thick-rimmed glasses and mixed gray-and-black hair. Her heart beat faster than it had in years. That's the book, she thought. That sho must be the book that I done sent off for.

She picked up the magazine and flipped the pages nonchalantly, but with eyes that focused on each picture and quickly soaked it in. She was almost ready to smile. Oh Lawd, she thought.

"Now, Mr. Sheriff, just what kind of trick you playin' on ole Granny? We already got one preacher, and you goes off and comes here with the picture of another preacher, and we don't need none. Now I knows Preacher Harris is gettin' old, but he ain't nearly as old as me now, is he? That is a preacher, ain't it, Sheriff?"

He jerked the magazine from her hand. "Yes, it's a preacher. But what do you know about it?"

"Now, Sheriff, I don't mean no disrespect and I'm sho tryin' to answer you just as quick as my ole head can come up with an answer, but I just don't rightly know what to say, Sheriff, 'cause I don't know what y'all mean."

"I mean that magazine, that goddamn *Ebony* Magazine."

"Ebb-ooo-nee. That the name of that there book, Sheriff?"

"Of course it is, woman, and you better come up with a better answer than you're givin' me or I'll see to it that you never get a year older." He reached for her hair but there wasn't enough for him to grab. "Goddammit, nigger, why don't you people have more hair?"

The baby started crying.

"Now look what you done, Sheriff. You done woke the baby up and after I been tryin' and tryin' to get her to go to sleep. Mrs. Matthews says she's had a bad bellyache and I finally got her to feel a little better—and besides, I don't know nothin' 'bout that book noways. You know I can't read."

"That's right," Mr. Howard said. "Can't none of them read except the preacher and the boys in the post office, and they can't read nothin' but names and numbers. She don't know nothin' about it, Sheriff."

"Well how did it get her name on it, then? You tell me that. How did it get to her in the first place? Bertha, if I find out you know how to read and you know what this is all about, you know what I'm gonna do to you, don't you?"

Granny laughed softly. "Mr. Sheriff, how'm I ever gonna learn to read? I ain't done nothin' but wash clothes and take care of babies all my life. You know I can't read none, Sheriff. I'm sorry, Mr. Sheriff. I wished I could if that would help you, but I can't even read the Bible."

"How them niggers up north know you down here, then?"

She got to her feet, placed the baby in a basket, and turned to face the sheriff. "Sheriff, you remember a long time ago when my granddaughter's husband—it was Big Jesse, that who it was—got in some trouble with you, and everyone said he left outta here for the north?"

The sheriff gritted his teeth. His facial muscles contracted spastically.

"Well, now, Sheriff, that's the only person in the world knows there's a Granny Jacobs here, unlessen it's some white folks who moved on up north and was just tryin' to be nice because I taken care of their babies. I never was no too smart, Mr. Sheriff, but I knows you figure it all out for me. I can't help it if that's my name, now, can I?"

"Come on," the sheriff said, getting into his car. "I can tell you one thing, Bertha, you ain't gonna see none of them pictures as long as I'm alive. I don't know who sent it to you, but you'll never get a chance to see it. You understand that?"

"Yes, suh, Mr. Sheriff, and the Lawd bless you for not hurtin' ole Granny."

The car sped off, leaving Granny standing in the dust, wiping at the tears that worked their way slowly down her fat cheeks.

⌇ *Eight*

THE NEGRO MAGAZINE stirred up more excitement than the white people of Jacobs County had seen in years. The day after it arrived an angry crowd gathered on the steps of the courthouse and demanded to see it. Some of the men refused to believe that such a magazine existed. Others felt that even if it did exist, Negroes surely didn't live as well as the magazine said.

"It's a plot by them northern nigger-lovers. They're just trying to turn our niggers against us," one man said.

The few who did believe the stories related about the magazine, now grown to ridiculous proportions, pretended not to believe. It was not healthy to go around saying that Negroes in the north lived better than many whites in the south. And those few who knew it was true stayed away from the town square. Mr. Jacobs didn't go to his bank for three days. There were too many questions being asked.

The sheriff realized that something had to be done to stop

the people from discussing the magazine. He knew that sooner or later they would decide that the conditions it showed really existed and that some Negroes up north did live better than the whites of Jacobs County. Once they reached this conclusion they would march to the colored section, armed with their fury, and with ropes and weapons, and, like a frightened and confused pack of ignorant animals, would begin a series of lynchings that might last for days.

The sheriff didn't mind an occasional grudge lynching—he had led many of them—but a mass lynching could get out of hand. The last one, ten years ago, had been set off when one of the town's more respected women committed suicide after bearing a baby that was thought to be colored, and ended with the death of many of the Negroes who had been trained to perform special jobs. When this sort of thing happened, the businessmen had to train new personnel, and they were always displeased with the sheriff as a result.

But this time luck was with the sheriff, and by the end of the day he had turned the whole episode into a comedy.

"Now you just tell me," he said, standing on the bumper of his squad car. "Just who is the joke really on? They sent that nigger magazine down here, and ain't nobody can read it but us, and we sure ain't black."

The crowd of thirty men roared with laughter.

"Hey, Sheriff," one man called out. "Why don't we teach them niggers to read so's they'll know what they're missing?"

"That's not a bad idea," said the sheriff. "Maybe if we start now we might be able to find one smart enough so's we could teach him to read sometime in the next hundred or so years." He threw his head back and laughed a loud horse laugh, just as the sheriff before him had laughed, and every sheriff the people of Jacobs County had ever known. It was a laugh Negroes had grown to fear. It was a laugh white people respected. It was a laugh white children tried to imitate, for it was obvious to them that the laugh made the sheriff, and no man in the county could be considered for the position unless he first was a man who laughed like a sheriff.

"Now you people go on home and let me get to work," the sheriff said. "You know I'll be working night and day trying to find one we can teach to read."

But in the Negro quarters there was no laughter. There was general unrest now that there was reason to believe the world outside of Jacobs County was better than even the white people had imagined. They were confused. They had been conditioned to accept without question the word of their white masters, but their make-up also demanded that they respect older people, as children must always respect adults, so they simply had to believe Granny Jacobs. Everyone knew she had never told a lie in her life, and, after all, she was almost as old as Jacobsville.

Negroes in the cotton fields, in the barns, and in the big warehouse at the end of the square, and even those working in and around Mr. Jacobs' house, were leaving work at the end of a long day with a quick step, hurrying away from the white man so they could get back to their own people and talk about the Negroes up north who lived in fine houses. They weren't singing so much any more, and they had begun talking to each other, standing straight up and actually carrying on a conversation, just as Mr. Jacobs did with the men who worked in his bank.

These were indeed strange times. There hadn't been a fight in days. They were beginning to feel a responsibility to one another; they were thinking more and more as one mind. They had been sprinkled with a little knowledge, and now, overnight, they were ravenously sucking in every bit of information they could get about their country. And with this thirst came a certain brightness in their eyes; they were becoming aware of themselves as human beings and beginning to question, though only among themselves, some of the ways they had always accepted on faith. They were coming alive.

They wanted to know more about the magazine, about the bright cars and fine clothes, the beautiful black women and the big houses, and especially about the schools, where colored boys and girls and young men and women learned about things the Jacobs County Negroes didn't understand, but knew must be worth learning if the colored folks up north bothered about them.

Perhaps the most important reason for their new-found unity was their secret. Twenty-five years ago they had had a secret, and Granny Jacobs had figured in that one, too. And now once again her name was used to bring her people together. The whites didn't know that Granny had seen more in the magazine than she had revealed to the sheriff, or that at one time she had had personal contact with the outside world. And although the Negroes might have told on someone else, they wouldn't tell on Granny because she was the noble old woman they all wanted to be like; she had that trace of dignity that made her different from everyone else in Jacobsville, black or white, and once again she had to be protected.

They visited Granny Jacobs in such large numbers that she had to come outside and talk to them. They wanted to hear her tell what she had seen in the magazine. And Granny Jacobs sat on her stoop and spoke in quiet tones about the wonders of the world outside of Jacobsville.

"And do y'all know that in that there magazine there was colored folks livin' in houses biggern Mr. Jacobs' house? And they had other colored folks workin' for 'em, in fancy clothes like they used to wear here when I was just a little girl."

"But Granny," a wiry youth asked, "can they really do anything they wants to do and ain't no white man stops 'em from comin' and goin'?"

"That's right, son. Even over in the town of Minnott they comes and goes. It was one of them colored families over there that took Little Jesse up north so's he could be a free man, God bless their soul."

"Well, why don't they help us, then?" a voice called out loudly.

"Now don't start no hollerin', son, or you bring the sheriff down on our necks as fast as ants gets to molasses. They don't help us none 'cause they can't. It seems to me—now I don't know for sho—but it kinda looks like this here State of Mississippi is real special, 'cause ain't nobody never been big enough to tell these here white folks what they should do. I sort of guess now it wouldn't do no good noways, 'cause these white folks here just keep on doin' what they wants to do anyhow, and that's what happened to us. We been born down here where nobody can help us. I kinda reckon some of them white people up north might want to help if they knew about us, but they don't know we's down here. They don't know we still slaves."

"They knows, Granny," a young man said. "They knows and they don't give a damn what happens to us 'cause we just black. I say we oughta kill 'em all off and leave this place for the snakes. Ain't nobody gonna help us but us, so why not just kill 'em and get where we can live like people?"

Preacher Harris interrupted. "Just how far you think you get before them state troopers with them pretty uniforms run you down and stick you in jail? Maybe none of them white folks up north knows we here, but the white folks in Mississippi knows we here, and if we kills these white folks the other ones will sho 'nuf kill us."

"Not all of us," the man insisted. "Some's bound to get up north. They can't put us all in jail."

"They won't put none of us in jail," said Preacher Harris. "They'd get the hounds out and they'd come from every county in Mississippi to hunt us down. And when they caught up with us they wouldn't say nothin' about no jail. No, suh, they'd start shootin' and wouldn't stop 'til the last Jacobs County colored man was dead, so dead even the worms won't want him."

It soon became apparent to Preacher Harris that he could not control the young men by reading the Bible, and he feared they might do something rash and bring all of white Jacobs County down on them. They had organized themselves and selected Josh Black as their leader. Josh was short, but strong enough to break the back of the biggest man in Jacobsville. He had been trained to wrestle by the sheriff, and he had never been beaten. The sheriff had made good money on Josh, and as a reward he made him "Head Cleaner-Upper" of the jail. There wasn't a man in town who knew the sheriff better than Josh. There wasn't a man more suited for leadership. There wasn't a man better qualified to kill the sheriff. Once the sheriff was no longer a threat, they would see to it that the old people and children got out of the county, and then they would be able to devise a plan of action and force the white people to free them.

But Preacher Harris called a special prayer meeting at the church, because he and Granny Jacobs had decided they must try to persuade the young men to wait until they had first tried to get help by writing a letter to the President.

Josh sat in the first pew. He was flanked on each side by five young men who had met with him in the woods on several occasions, trying to develop a plan to save their people, and who were angry by now because their meetings had brought no results. For all their efforts they still didn't know what to do. They were tired of waiting, and they wanted to take some kind of action *now*, but they were afraid to act in any way that might provoke violence, because they were not ready to fight. They felt it would have been much easier to take their grievances to the sheriff or Mr. Jacobs and let them work it out, as they always did. They didn't want much, only to be told the truth, and to be allowed to leave Jacobs County if they wished. But the magazine was proof that the whites had lied in the past, and in all probability they would go on lying. The men were angry because of "the white lie," as they had come to call it. They were angry because they realized they had been wronged. They were angry because they had too few weapons. And they were angry because they were exhausted from this new way of living, this business of thinking and trying to do things for themselves.

Josh listened to Preacher Harris for a while, but then he began to dream about the magazine, and then about the sheriff; and when he looked up at Preacher Harris again he saw the tall, heavy man in black, but heard a white man's voice coming from his mouth:

"You're a strong boy, Josh. You gotta lift more 'cause you're stronger than the rest of the niggers. Now lift, boy, lift!" It was Mr. Sheehan, the warehouse man, who had made him as strong as he was; making his loads heavier and heavier, until

Josh was finally doing the work of two men although he was only twelve. And when he faltered, when he broke something or passed out from exhaustion, it was Mr. Sheehan who tied him to a post with his hands behind his back and punched him until his fists were as bloody and scarred as Josh's face. And only when Josh pretended to be unconscious would Mr. Sheehan stop, exhausted and satisfied.

Josh ran his hand over his face, tracing the scars with his fingertips, and then he touched his broad, misshapen nose; and he realized the only man he had ever hated was Mr. Sheehan. I ain't nothin' but an ugly ape, he thought, but I'm still livin', Mr. Sheehan, and you ain't. I'm still livin', and, the Lawd willin', I'm gonna be free, and I hope you turn flip-flops in yo' ole stinkin' grave. I hate you so much I almost want to pray you don't go to heaven, but I ain't got no need to worry none 'bout that 'cause you sho ain't in no heaven.

But he didn't hate the sheriff. He and the sheriff were friends. The sheriff had fed and clothed him and always told him the truth. 'Cep 'bout them colored folks up north, he thought. He didn' tell me the truth 'bout 'em. Oh, Lawd, why'd he have to lie this time? We suppose' to be friends and friends don't lie.

"We're partners, boy," the sheriff had said. Josh was fifteen then and already the strongest man in town. "You wrestle for me and I'll give you a job in the jail. I'll take care of you, Josh boy, but you gotta work hard."

"Yes, suh," Josh said.

"Now what I want you to do is listen to everything I tell you, boy."

"Yes, suh, Mr. Sheriff."

"And if you do good, I just might make you a colored deputy when you grow up. How's that sound to you?"

"That's nice."

"Yes, sir, boy, you and me is partners. How'd you like to sleep right here in the jail?"

His eyes sparkled. "Me, Mr. Sheriff?"

"That's right, boy."

"Yes, suh." He pointed to a space between the desk and the wall. "That be just fine right there, Mr. Sheriff."

"No, boy. I told you, you and me is partners. How'd you like to sleep in the cell in that *bed*?"

Josh was beside himself with excitement. "Me?"

"That's right. Just you."

"But that's Mr. Deputy Bob's bed."

"We'll get him a new bed. Now don't you worry about it, Josh boy. It's all right. The deputy won't mind. He knows we can't have you livin' out there with them other niggers. We gotta see to it that you eat and drink the right kind of food, boy." He slapped Josh on the back and Josh smiled. "Oh, no, it's gonna be different for you now, Josh. Can't have you out there with the rest of them, fightin' and maybe gettin' your throat cut."

"But my people don't fight me, Mr. Sheriff. Nobody never fights me. I ain't never had no fight in my whole natural life."

"I know, boy, but it's different now. Understand?"

Josh nodded, then cocked his head to the side and waited to have it explained to him as he always did.

"You don't know what I mean, do you, boy?"

He shook his head.

"Now I'm gonna explain it to you and I want you to listen."

"Yes, suh."

"Now you better learn it."

"I sho will, Mr. Sheriff."

"I ain't sayin' it again. And if you don't learn it I'm gonna have to beat you. You don't want me to beat you, do you?"

"No, *suh*."

"And I don't want to beat you, boy. You believe that now, don't you?"

"Oh, I always believes you, Mr. Sheriff. Everybody does. Everybody always believes you. That's one thing folks always sayin' about you: If you says something, you means it and that's the natural truth."

"Now you can go out there to nigger-town sometimes. Maybe once a week you can go out there when you feel the need, but I don't want you livin' there 'cause you bettern all them niggers. You bettern all them put together now, boy. Why—next to a white man, I guess you must be the best boy in town!"

His chest swelled with pride.

The sheriff continued. "Why, when I get through with you, you'll even be bettern a house nigger. And just between you and me, Josh, that's gettin' mighty close to white folks. So you see why I don't want you stayin' out in nigger-town. You're just too good for them animals. Now you go on over there and try out the bed and see how you like it."

Josh hesitated.

"Go on. It's yours. And you can even have that sheet and that blanket!"

". . . and we don't want no killin'," he heard Preacher Harris say. "Not by us and not by them. The Lawd is on our side and we . . ."

Josh closed his eyes and cupped his face in his hands. Killin', killin', he thought. White folks always killin' somethin'. Like that boy I went into the woods and got for the sheriff 'cause all the white folks was scared 'cause that boy was clean outta his head, smilin' back at that white girl just 'cause she smiled that way to him. I coulda smiled at her and even done more, but that's 'cause I was the sheriff's nigger. But that boy didn't have no kind of sense to think he could smile that way, even if he was big as a tree. And the sheriff said they wasn't gonna do nothin' to him. "We just gonna put him in jail next to you for a time, Josh." That's what he said so's I'd go get him. And no soonern I brung the boy down, they was all over him, kickin' and hittin' and cuttin' at him. Oh Lawd, they sho ruint that boy. Wasn't 'nuf left for the rats. And when I tried to stop it and reminded the sheriff what he said, he just hauled off and cracked me one with that shotgun and laid me out cold as a possum.

My folks didn' even talk to me after that—not for a long

time. How long ago was that? I been the sheriff's nigger, oh, must be 'bout ten years now. Sho, it's ten years if it's a day. Least I think it's ten years. And that didn't happen no too long ago—maybe four or five years. They didn' have to kill that boy. Didn' do nothin' ain't been goin' on since I was a baby.

He lied to me just like always. Been lyin' and lyin' all the time, and lyin' and lyin' some mo'. What he say when I come right out and ask him 'bout the magazine? He say it's a lie. Say it's people up north tryin' to ruin our country. Say it was just propa-somethin', whatever that means, and niggers up north starvin' in the streets and gettin' shot down and runned over, and freezin' in the winter 'cause they ain't got no clothes. And say he don't want me askin' no mo' questions like that and if I do he gonna crack me over the head. And then he tell me if I hear anything in nigger-town to come and tell him. Must think I'm a fool. I told him somethin' once—no mo'. Not no mo', Mr. Sheriff—I don't believe you.

"Horace says he throws the bags on the mail truck that takes the mail out of here to the train station," Preacher Harris said, speaking so softly now that he could not be heard beyond the third pew. "And you know I'm sho gonna write a good letter. I give him the letter and when he comes to the bag marked C-H-I-C-A-G-O he puts the letter in there, and when the bag gets to Chicago they sees it's suppose' to go to Washington where the President lives, and they sends it right on to him, and he gets it and sees how they treats us, and he sends his army down to free us."

"And if he don't," Josh said, "we will!"

That night Preacher Harris and Granny sat at the worn pine desk in his office as he wrote and rewrote the letter to the President. In all his sixty years he had never been called upon to do anything that took so much courage. He had been a good preacher. There was no question about that. He had given his flock the word of God, and taught them to live not for the things the white man had but for the everlasting life of God's kingdom. He had never deviated from his teachings, and now, more than ever before, he was leading them away from sin.

"Lawd give me strength," he said softly as he tore up one page and started again. "Lawd give me strength."

The warm sun was coming through the stained-glass window above his desk as he read the letter over to himself for the fifth and last time.

Dear Mr. President,

You don't know me but I'm Preacher George Harris and me and Granny Jacobs, she's sitting next to me as I write this letter are writing you to tell you about us here in Jacobs County Mississippi. Granny subscribed to a colored magazine because her great-grandson was to be in it and he is up in Chicago and has writ a book and the ebony magazine has taken pictures of him and his wife and children and Granny wanted to see it and Mr. Howard he the postman in charge of the post office and the sheriff took it. The sheriff said she can't never read none of them magazines. Granny wanted for me to write you so she could see her grandson in that there book. The young colored folks are mad down here. The young people say you forgot all about us down here. I say you don't know about us. I is writin to tell you about us because if you don't come down here or send that army down to do something to free my people they is going to kill every white man and every white woman and every white child in Jacobs County. We slaves down here Mr. President. We been slaves ever since I can remember and I been here sixty years and Granny Jacobs been here more than eighty years and she still a slave. The sheriff and Mr. Jacobs and the sheriffs deputies make us work in the fields and in the house and in the warehouse and on folks farms and in the post office and in the stores and in the jails and everywhere and ain't never paid us no money cep when we ask for food or for some clothes or things like that and they don't let us leave Jacobs County. Ifen one of us tries to leave we gets kilt just as quick as swattin a fly we gets kilt. We just found out that colored folks aint slaves nowheres else cep here and we want you to free us. Ifen you don't come the young men is gonna kill the white people and take over the town so please come and save us. Please come and help deliver my people Mr. President. May the Lawd give you what you need to help us that he has done give my people to live as long as they has down here with this satan. My name is George Harris and I live in Jacobsville and everybody here knows me.

Ifen you come you better not let the sheriff know what you comin for cause he sure to kill some of my colored folks and you better come quick cause next week is all the time they givin you and they means to do what they says.

He pasted a stamp in place, addressed the envelope, and slipped it into his pocket.

"Come on, Granny. It's time you went home. The letter's all finished and I'm takin' it to Horace so's he can send it off." He took Granny's arm and she noticed his hand was wet and trembling.

"You ain't got nothin' to be 'fraid of, Preacher Harris," Granny said softly. "You a good man and the good man is always on the side of the Lawd."

Nine

A WEEK LATER TWO strange white men drove into Jacobs-ville and inquired at the filling station about accommodations for the night. When they were told there was no motel they looked at each other in amazement and asked where visitors stayed.

"Well," the attendant said, "we don't have that many visitors nohow, bein' as we're off the main road and folks just don't bother to come around here. Ain't nothin' here for them to come to see." He took his eyes off the nozzle and discovered the rear window. He ran his forefinger over the window, turned his head, and called, "Nigger! Get out here and wipe this here car off. You hear me, now?"

An elderly Negro limped out of the garage, wiping his oil-stained hands on his pants. "I'm comin', Mr. Mo'. Didn't know you had no car out here, suh."

"Don't give me no lip. Now I don't want to have to call you no more today." He never once looked at the Negro. He kept his eyes on the meter. Then he turned to face the two men. "That's one thing we got more than enough of. We got niggers everywhere. We got niggers standing on top of niggers."

The northerners were embarrassed. "How's the fishing around here?" one of the gentlemen asked. "I've been told you can catch some big ones."

"Fishin' ain't no good no more. Niggers. They fish from sunup to sundown. Don't believe in throwin' nothin' back. Anything they catch they eat. Don't matter none how small it is. They sure can live on fish. Yes, sir, that's one thing we got a lot of."

"How far is the lake?" the other man asked.

"What for? I told you ain't no fish in it. Hurry up with that window, nigger. Look at him. I don't know why he don't die. He must be almost as old as that Granny. Don't know why he don't go ahead and die so's I can get me a new mechanic. He's a good one, though."

"But the fishing is good somewhere around here, isn't it?" the man said, trying to change the subject.

"I told you it ain't. You Yankees don't hear too good, do you? They catch the fish as soon as they're big enough to get a hook in their mouth."

"But I thought you said you had a lot of fish?"

"Ain't got no fish. Got a lot of niggers. Ain't got no fish, though. You know there's ten of them to one of us right here. But they ain't quite right so it don't matter none. Now if it was ten of me to one of them—" He turned to face the Negro for the first time and suddenly grew tense. The old man had finished with the windows and was standing by the car smiling, as if waiting for a command to move. "That's a good job, boy. Now go back and get to work on that car and don't come out 'til it's fixed."

The mechanic hurried into the garage.

Once he was out of sight the attendant smiled and said, "Yes, sir, if it was ten of me to one of them, boy oh boy, boy oh boy . . ."

"How much do we owe you?" the driver asked.

"You from Maryland, huh? Well, now, that ain't north, is it? You sure sound like Yankees, though. Sound just like foreigners. That's three dollars and fifteen cents."

The passenger paid the attendant. The driver got into the car and started the engine.

"If there's anything you want to know about fishin' you better ask the sheriff. He knows all about everything in this town. You best talk to him because you might end up on somebody's property and find yourself in jail. The jail's right over there. Better turn around and stop there first and if you don't you still better turn around 'cause you headed right for niggertown and they get real wild down there when it's hot like this. Sheriff finds people down there all the time with their—well, with all kinds of things wrong with 'em."

"Thanks," the driver said. The car pulled off and headed for the Negro section. The attendant watched it go out of sight hidden behind a cloud of dirt as it left the blacktop at the edge of the town's business district. He stood watching the dust for several minutes and then he walked slowly across the street to the sheriff's office.

Ten

THE TWO MEN drove along the dirt road for one mile, until they came to a fork. The road to the left led to a white mansion off in the distance, standing on a hill from which it commanded a view of the entire town. The road leading up the hill to the house was lined with willows, and a beautifully landscaped garden swept down and away from the house in a series of giant steps, until it ran into the cotton field at the bottom of the hill, some seven levels beneath the house. They turned right, almost certain that they would arrive in the Negro section. After a short distance they saw two Negro women walking on the side of the road. The driver stopped.

"Good morning," he said.

The women smiled and exposed their rotten teeth; then their smiles vanished and were replaced with dumb, lifeless stares, as if they had smiled only on command.

"Can you tell me where we can locate Reverend Harris and Granny Jacobs?"

The women pointed in the direction they had come from and flashed their mechanical smiles on and off again.

"Thank you," the driver said, putting the car in gear and starting up.

"Are they always that frightened?" the passenger said.

"Just about," said the driver. "I've seen the same lifeless faces all over the south, and even up north in the big cities, in the ghettos. I guess if you try hard enough you can beat even a strong man down to the level of a plow horse."

They continued slowly down the winding dirt road, through the forest, on their way to the Negro quarters. Finally the woods opened up and they saw in the huge dirt clearing ahead of them a cluster of one-room shacks, each one scarcely bigger than an outhouse; dried, cracking, decaying, paintless wooden structures, whose tarpaper roofs were patched with more dried timber, or with cardboard or tin cans. Some of the buildings had sheets of plastic for windows; some were fitted with wooden shutters that were swung open to let the daylight in; some were boarded up; and a few were nothing more than four walls, a roof, and a door, with no windows. There was no grass and there were no visible property lines, and in some cases a newer house that had been built too close to a sagging older one was now serving to support it. There was no old southern charm here. Everything was gray. Everything was dirty. Everything was very old and very worn. Children ran back and forth across the small opening that lay between the two rows of houses and served as a road. When they saw the car coming they gathered together in small groups and stared with sad, frightened eyes at the two strange-looking white men.

The driver stopped the car. "Can one of you kids tell me where Granny Jacobs lives?" he asked.

A little tot started forward. An older girl restrained her and then pointed. The others remained motionless, almost to the point of holding their breath.

"How far?"

"Way down," she said. "First house."

The children grouped closer together.

The driver smiled. "Thank you, young lady."

The children smiled and scattered.

As the car crept slowly along, Negroes began to appear in front of houses, beside them, at the open windows; men, women, and children seemed to materialize before them. The street that had at first been almost vacant was now swarming with people, all headed in the direction of Granny's house. These people, who had never known the meaning of the word resistance, were marching to Granny's house to protect her from the white men. They had heard how the sheriff had treated her and they had decided that she should not be mistreated again.

"If that cracker touches one hair of that ole woman's head again, I'll break his goddamn back," Josh had said. The other men had drawn strength from his words and pledged that they too would fight. And now, because white men were asking where the old woman lived, word had gone out that someone was after Granny. Mothers had stopped washing and feeding their babies, little boys had ended their games, young and old men had left the fields and were running to the first house from the cotton field, where Granny sat tending three white children, who ran into the woods with a group of Negro children.

"Y'all don't go too far in them woods," the strangers heard her say as they drove up.

They pulled the car off the road and got out. "You must be Mrs. Jacobs," the driver said warmly.

She turned slowly and was startled to see two such tall, handsome white men standing there smiling, with the people crowding around them. She smiled and said, "Guess I can't fool nobody, even if I try. Yes, suh, I's Granny Jacobs."

"Good morning. I'm Federal Marshal Ernest Wright," the driver said, extending his hand.

Granny shook hands with him, but a look of bewilderment crept over her face.

"The President sent me," he said.

"Thank you, Jesus," Granny said, smiling and pumping away at his arm. "Thank you, Jesus."

"The President sent 'em," someone in the crowd shouted, and a spontaneous roar went up.

"Some of y'all folks go get Preacher Harris and Josh."

"He's comin', Granny," someone yelled.

Then another voice called out, "Josh can't come. He's with the sheriff."

Ernest Wright turned to look for his companion, who was being treated to one hundred or so vigorous handshakes.

"This is Mr. Fred Worthington, Mrs. Jacobs. He's a postal inspector who was also sent here by the President. Among other things, we're going to make sure that you receive all your mail."

Granny walked into the crowd, pushing people aside, and shook hands with the other white man.

Three young men appeared, carrying chairs over their heads. "Watch out," one of them shouted, and they placed the chairs in a circle in the center of the road. The two white men seated Granny and then themselves.

"Now all you young men come close, so's you can bring what's said back to Josh," Granny said.

The crowd, which now numbered well over two hundred, backed off to clear a place. The men came forward and ringed the chairs.

Granny said, "Now all y'all sit down so's the other folks can hear."

"You go ahead and tell it like it is, Granny," a woman called out.

"As God is my witness, I ain't gonna tell no lies," said Granny. "But we's waitin' for Preacher Harris before we get started."

"'Scuse me, suh," a young man standing nearby said. "Where's the army?"

"We came to look things over to see just what state they're in."

"I can tell you what state they's in. They's in a state of slavery."

"Don't you let the sheriff hear you talkin' like that," an older man said.

"Yeah," the young man said sadly. "They didn't bring no army with 'em and we still here in Jacobsville, and the sheriff—"

"Y'all shut up and let Granny talk," a voice called out. "She can tell it bettern all y'all put together. Besides, the sheriff ain't 'bout to bother her."

Preacher Harris arrived, out of breath and mopping the sweat from his forehead with one of his newer handkerchiefs. After he had been introduced to the visitors, he said a long prayer of thanks, during which another chair was brought out. Then he seated himself, and Granny Jacobs slowly and methodically gave the two gentlemen a complete history of the slave story of Jacobs County. She was the archives of the town. When she had difficulty remembering a name, however, she would call out, "Who was that boy, now?" and someone from the crowd would furnish the name. Marshal Wright interrupted occasionally to clarify a point. When he had finished writing what he wanted in the book, he would say, "Go ahead, please, Mrs. Jacobs," and she would take up from where she had left off.

Within an hour the marshal and the inspector had enough information to justify their continued presence in Jacobs County. Marshal Wright began calling people up from the crowd and interrogating them. At first they were hesitant to talk, but a few words of encouragement from Granny soon dispelled their fears, and from then on the marshal couldn't call them up fast enough. They had gone through some thirty interviews when suddenly a man came running down out of the hills.

"Sheriff's comin'. Sheriff's comin'," he said, and the crowd, which had been silent except for the occasional crying of a baby, exploded into motion. Women screamed, picked up their children, and ran. The people farthest away from Granny and in the path of the automobile vanished into houses. The men who had gathered nearest the chairs held fast, and those who had been undecided just stood their ground, afraid to move, afraid not to move.

The sheriff arrived in a cloud of dust, the back end of the car skidding across the road. Two of the deputies and the old fat sheriff were out of the automobile before it stopped; the third deputy followed as soon as he had set the brakes, running to catch up. Their guns were drawn, and they swung them to clear a path for the sheriff.

"What the hell's goin' on here," the sheriff shouted, working his way through to Granny Jacobs.

Preacher Harris jumped to his feet and began smiling and bowing.

"Afternoon, Sheriff," Granny said. "This here is a federal marshal. The President sent him."

"President of what?" the sheriff said sarcastically.

Marshal Wright produced his credentials and handed them to the sheriff without saying a word.

"This don't give you no right to come down here and cause no riot," the sheriff said, returning the little black folder.

"There's no difficulty here," said Marshal Wright. "We were having a nice peaceful talk."

The sheriff was at a loss for words. He knew things were not going as they should, but he wasn't sure what authority the man from Washington had or how he could use it. There had never been a problem like this for a sheriff of Jacobs County, and although he wanted to put the outsiders in jail or run them out of town, he was afraid to antagonize the federal government.

"Well," he said finally, "I better stay here with you to make sure none of these nigras hurt you. You don't know these people like I do. Why, they'd cut your throat in a minute if I was to leave you alone here with them." He smiled, satisfied that he had said the right thing.

The Negroes had remained perfectly still since the sheriff arrived and the marshal knew there would be no use trying to get information from them while the sheriff was there to intimidate them with his presence.

"Very well," said Marshal Wright. "Then perhaps you can have one of your men drive Mr. Worthington to the post office so he can make his inspection today. That way we can get through all our business in one day."

"Huh? Why's he got to go to the post office?"

"He's a postal inspector."

"I thought you was both federal marshals?"

"I'm the marshal. He's a postal inspector."

"Oh, I see," said the sheriff, scratching his head, trying desperately to find some way out of this grave situation. He had seen the federal marshals in Oxford in 1962 and he didn't want any in Jacobs County. And then his southern charm went to work. He smiled and said, "Man oh man, you fellas sure do sneak up on a man. I'm Sheriff Pitch." He and the marshal shook hands and the Negroes looked at them suspiciously. "These are my three deputies. I was just thinkin', we could put you up for the night somewhere in town—or maybe Mr. Jacobs would like to have you for guests. Mighty fine house he's got up there. Let you know what real southern hospitality is like and then first thing in the mornin' I can take you over to the post office and sort of take personal charge—make sure you see everything you came to see before you leave. How's that sound to you?"

"No, I think I'd better go now," the inspector said.

"I appreciate your offer," Marshal Wright said, "but we have to keep moving because we have other stops to make."

"It's a routine investigation on my part," Worthington told the sheriff. "The post office isn't that big. I should be through in about an hour. One of your men could drop me there and return for you."

The sheriff knew they were lying, but there was nothing he could do. "Tell you what I'll do. I'll leave my deputies here with you and I'll drive this gentleman in myself. And when you finish you can bring my deputies in with you."

"All right," said Marshal Wright. "Anything you say, Sheriff."

"Sure sorry you can't stay over, though."

"So are we. But you know how it is when you've got a schedule to keep."

When they reached the post office there was a Negro loading mailbags on a truck out front.

"Do you work here?" Worthington asked the man before the sheriff had a chance to speak.

"Yes, suh," the Negro said, flashing that patented smile.

"How long have you worked here?"

"Oh . . ." The man fingered his chin whiskers and looked at the sky, searching his mind for an answer. "A long time," he said finally.

"I see. How much do you make a year?"

"Sometimes they gives me maybe a dollar a day and sometimes I don't make so much."

The sheriff started for the door.

"Just a minute, Sheriff," the inspector said. "I'll go in with you in a second."

Sheriff Pitch stood awkwardly at the door, unable to warn the postmaster.

"Are you a regular or a substitute?" the inspector asked.

"Huh?"

"Never mind. Go on with your work. I want to see you before I leave, though."

"Yes, suh."

Inside, Worthington met the postmaster and was ushered through the building. He stopped and talked with each of the twenty Negroes, and was not surprised to find that none of them was employed by the government. Finally he turned to the postmaster and said, "How are these men paid and why are they here if they aren't employees?"

Sheriff Pitch interrupted. "Mr. Worthington, we got so many nigras here we just decided to let them help out and pay them something out of the city fund so they'll have food and something to do. The poor nigras would all starve if we didn't take them in like this. They ain't none too bright—like children, they are—but we take good care of them and they're happy as hell."

"That's right," the postmaster said. "They're happy, all right. Happiest people in the world."

Eleven

THAT AFTERNOON Marshal Wright and his companion left Jacobsville and met with five other marshals in a hotel room in Minnott, where they had a direct line to Washington. They reported their findings and received further instructions. They were to return to Jacobs County immediately and set up headquarters in Jacobsville somewhere between the Negro section and the white section. The postal inspector was to relieve the postmaster of his duties, and to stay on the job in Jacobsville until a formal investigation could be made. All white postal clerks were to be suspended indefinitely. The Negroes who had worked in the post office were to be given immediate civil-service status, and some arrangement would be made later to compensate them for the years of employment without adequate salaries. The entire operation was to be kept secret.

The President, that very evening, spent one hour on the telephone talking to the Governor of Mississippi. It was agreed that the situation in Jacobs County must be corrected, and that it was absolutely imperative that no one outside the county ever discover what had been going on there. They decided that six state troopers and six marshals would be stationed in Jacobsville until the crisis was over; the use of more men would make it impossible to keep the operation a secret.

The Governor was displeased to learn that the white postal employees would have to be discharged; when he insisted that they be kept on, the President agreed that they should be reinstated after a two-week suspension; all but the postmaster, who would have to be replaced. The Governor assured the President that he would talk with the sheriff, and impress upon him the importance of controlling the white minority, so that the minor problem in Jacobs County would not become a major crisis making imperative the use of federal troops. The President and the Governor were certain the Negroes would not cause any trouble.

The sheriff and Mr. Jacobs spent most of the night trying to persuade the Governor to postpone the drastic action the government planned to take until they had a chance to work out some means of changing things gradually, in a manner that would be more acceptable to the white citizens. Their telephone calls were made from Mr. Jacobs' house, and Sheriff Pitch used the extension phone, so that it was a three-way conversation.

"Gentlemen," the Governor finally said, "my hands are tied, and for the record I have to tell you to go along with the marshals. But if the people should decide to get a little rough, you couldn't possibly be expected to stop them. As I see it, if the people should decide to chase the niggers out—not all of them, just say a good portion of them, because as long as you have so damn many of them you'll have trouble—well, there just wouldn't be anything you could do. Nobody could blame you. And I'll stand behind you all the way. I don't think it would be wise to have any harm come to the marshals, though."

When the sheriff met with the marshals and troopers early the next morning, he presented the perfect image of an impartial, understanding, and co-operative police officer. The marshals had expected trouble later in the day, after the postal inspector dismissed the white employees, but the sheriff became a worker of miracles, traveling from house to house, talking with people and quieting their angry tempers. All that day the marshals sensed the tension and feared they might have to call for assistance should the white citizens be unable to control their tempers and resort to violence. But the day went smoothly—too smoothly, as if the entire town might explode at any minute. The marshals were glad to see night come.

The next morning, Marshal Wright was awakened by a marshal named Johnson who had been on watch the latter part of the night.

"There's something over here you ought to see, Mr. Wright," Johnson said.

They started walking away from the camp site toward a heavy cluster of bushes fifty yards away. "I heard something in the trees this way just about an hour before daybreak but I figured it was an animal of some kind," Johnson said. "When it got light I decided to walk up, and this is what I found." He parted the bushes, and Marshal Wright looked in and saw the mutilated bodies of three naked teen-age Negro girls lying side by side. The girls had obviously been raped many times, and then beaten beyond recognition. One of the girls was missing her left breast, another a hand. Their bodies were covered with coagulated blood, and in places white, jagged-edged bones had broken through the brown skin.

Marshal Wright turned away from the bodies after a quick examination, and he and Johnson started back to camp in silence. Finally he said, "Ever feel ashamed to be white, Johnson?"

"Not until now, sir."

"Me neither. And these are the bastards who go around saying the Negroes are savages."

Back at camp the other marshals were up and dressing. Marshal Wright began shouting instructions.

"Fahey, go get Granny Jacobs and Reverend Harris. Ask them to please come here. Goldberg, get that goddamn sheriff and bring him out here right away. And stick your gun in his ribs if you have to hurry him up. Wilson, I want you to wake up that spineless Jacobs, and bring him down to see what his neighbors left us during the night. Johnson! Get some blankets and cover those kids."

Marshal Goldberg was the first to return, with the sheriff riding next to him. Massaging his buttocks, the sheriff stepped out of the automobile.

"Boy oh boy, that's sure a rough-ridin' car. Seems to me the federal government oughta be able to get something a little more comfortable for you gentlemen to ride in. Fast little thing, though. Good mornin' there, Mr. Wright. It's an awful early hour to get a man out of his bed. Must really be important."

"It is," the marshal said drily. "Step over here a minute." They walked to the bodies, and the marshal removed the blankets.

"Oh," said the sheriff, with the appropriate amount of sadness in his voice. "That's a terrible thing for somebody to do."

"Any idea who?"

"Well, now, it seems to me there's a couple of colored boys that could do this kind of thing. Should of picked them boys up a long time ago. And to think they'd do a thing like this to their own kind."

"It's hard to believe that Negroes would have done this."

"Never can tell about these nigras. I've known them to do a lot worse."

"I'll make a bargain with you, Sheriff. You work on it, and if you don't get any results before nightfall, I'll flood this county with marshals and tear it apart piece by piece until I find the bastards who did this. That's the bargain. You've got until night to get some results, and I suggest you start looking among the whites!"

Sheriff Pitch had gone when Granny, Preacher Harris, and Josh arrived.

"I'm sorry to have to bring you people out this early, but we've had some difficulty."

"Y'all find them three girls that didn't come home last night?" Josh said drily.

Marshal Wright was taken by complete surprise. "Yes, as a matter of fact we did. But how'd you know about it?"

"We knew," said Granny sadly. "We all knew."

Preacher Harris nodded his head.

Josh said, "Mr. White Man, when you been livin' here all yo' life, you knows. And when three colored girls shows up missin', you just prays that when you finds 'em they still alive. We been out lookin' for 'em all night. They must of took 'em way over the other side of the county to do it, 'cause we looked all night long."

"Johnson said he heard noises before dawn, but he thought they were made by animals."

"It was animals all right," Josh said. "Two-legged white ones."

"I had the sheriff out here—laid the law down to him. I think he's going to do something about this."

"Ain't gonna do nothin'," said Josh.

"Well, if he doesn't, I will. I have to make a report to Washington, and I'll get permission to bring in more marshals—and the F.B.I. too, now that this has happened. We'll catch the animals who did this. We'll catch every one of them."

"Ain't gonna do no good!" Josh slammed his fist down on the hood of the car so hard it made a dent. "You can't do a damn thing about it." Tears clouded his eyes, and he turned away, back toward the Negro section. "Ain't a thing you can do about it."

"Just a minute. I know you don't trust me and I can't say I blame you, but I promise you that I'll get the people responsible for this."

Josh turned back to the marshal. "All right! You catch 'em, here. And what's that gonna mean? Nothin'. You put 'em in jail and pick a white jury and have a white judge and white lawyers, and they get off. Let me tell you somethin', Mr. White Man. Ain't no white man never set one foot in that there jail for nothin' he did to a colored man. Never! Not for robbin' him and not for beatin' him and not for takin' his woman and not for even killin' him. Down here a colored man ain't worth half as much as a bad hound." He turned away finally, this time, and marched off.

$\backsim$ *Twelve*

Now sheriff pitch, like most of his neighbors, had never had much education; he hadn't been to college, he hadn't even been to high school, and one would have expected, as the marshals mistakenly did, that such a man would be no match for a group of well-organized college graduates. Had the marshals given their role in Jacobsville more thought, they might have been able to foresee what was to happen. But they didn't, and so it came about that Marshal Wright found himself that night securely locked behind bars in the Jacobsville jail, along with the other five marshals and the postal inspector. The vulgar, illiterate sheriff had outwitted the entire United States government because all the time he had known something they didn't know. He knew he was at war with the Yankee forces; he knew he was fighting the same war his great-grandfather had fought.

Outsmarting the marshals had been so easy that the sheriff was almost disappointed. He had expected some resistance.

At three o'clock he had sent word to Marshal Wright that he had a man in custody as one of the murder suspects, and would like the marshal's assistance. Wright and two other marshals rode into town, walked into the jail, and were disarmed at gun point by the sheriff. The rest of the marshals were brought in by the state troopers and similarly disarmed, with no more resistance than a mild verbal protest. The postal inspector, of all people, sensed that something was wrong. When the two deputies came for him he resisted until one well-placed blow at the base of the skull rendered him unconscious.

It was now eight o'clock. It would be dark soon, and the sheriff and his deputies and three of the state troopers were preparing to leave the jail to join the other troopers and most of the town's white men at the fork in the road. From there, half of them would go to the church to get Preacher Harris and the other half would go after Granny Jacobs.

They were going to set an example for all Negroes the world over. They were going to roast Granny and Preacher Harris alive, slowly, as they would barbecue a hog, and then they were going to destroy every single possession owned by any Negro in Jacobs County. If they couldn't have their Negroes the way they wanted them, they didn't want them at all. So they were going to chase them out. They were going to set three thousand Negroes free, and those who wouldn't leave would die tonight.

"After tonight," the sheriff had said to one of his deputies earlier that day, "I don't want to see another black bastard in

Jacobs County ever again—not if I live to be five hundred years old."

Of course the marshals knew nothing about what was to happen that night. The sheriff had insisted right along that they had been incarcerated for their own protection and that he and the troopers, all by themselves, could handle any difficulties that might arise. He told them that the townspeople had massed and he would disperse the mob.

"Now I know these people," he said. "I'll stop them. They don't take no too kindly to you northerners trying to change their ways, and they'd shoot you just like you was niggers. It's for your own protection, boy, that we'll have to keep you locked up until this is all over."

"I'd suggest you keep going after you're finished with whatever you're going to do," Marshal Wright said angrily, "because you're the first one I'm coming after."

"No—I don't think you'll do that. The decent people here won't stand for their sheriff being put in jail by a Yankee. I don't think you'll do anything like that. Besides, you just better hope I come back, or you might not get out at all. Never can tell how an angry mob will act. Why, they might even decide to string me up. Some people just ain't got no gratitude. Here I'm tryin' to save your life and you're threatening me. Well, I can't stand around all day arguing with you. I got to get out and stop all the troubles you brought down here. C'mon boys, let's go to work. Now you just stay put 'til we get back."

Outside, the sheriff said, "Hurry up, now. We can't keep the people waitin' out there all night, can we?" He and his deputies and the three troopers got into the two squad cars at the curb in front of the jail.

"Sheriff!" Bobbie Joe Willis called, running across the street from his hardware-grocery store. "Wait a minute, now."

"Hurry up, Bobbie Joe," the sheriff said. "We got important business, boy."

"Now goddammit, Sheriff, I'm tired of this shit. Every time there's a lynchin' somebody breaks into my shed and steals something. Last time they took all the ropes and kerosene I had, and this time I go out back and I find the lock busted just like always and every stick of dynamite I own gone. Dammit, that stuff costs money, and they don't need dynamite just to string up a few niggers."

"Dynamite! You hear that, boys?" Sheriff Pitch said. "We might even have a big boom tonight." He patted Bobbie Joe on the back. "It'll show up out there. I'll ask the boys to put it back for you—well, most of it, anyway."

They waited impatiently for the sheriff to arrive. Nearly all of the town's four hundred white men were present. They passed whisky around and talked about lynchings over the years, keeping it cheerful and trying to shorten the wait. It was like a church picnic.

"Pa," a young straw-head boy about twelve said. "When we gonna start?"

"When the sheriff says we start," his father said.

"Why don't we just go on ahead and get them niggers now? Why we gotta wait for him, Pa?"

"'Cause."

"'Cause what, Pa?"

"'Cause we gotta do what he says. We gotta obey the law and we can't do nothin' 'til he says we can."

"Oh," the boy said.

The father turned to a friend and said apologetically, "It's his first real lynchin' and he ain't too bright about it yet."

The men laughed.

"Always wait for the sheriff," a man said, putting his arm around the boy's shoulder. "See, that way we don't never get the wrong one. We made that a law, so to speak, a long time ago, because we was lynchin' the wrong niggers right and left and Mr. Jacobs got mad as hell. So now we wait for the sheriff to tell us who it is. And he don't make no mistakes. But it don't matter none this time. You can take that shotgun of yours, boy, and just shoot all you want tonight."

The boy clutched his shotgun affectionately, and smiled.

A man climbed on top of a car and tried to get the attention of the crowd. "Listen to me a minute. Now we all know that this just might be the last time we have any fun like this. So I say we tell the sheriff that we wanta have somethin' real special tonight. Know what I mean?"

"You goddamn right we know what you mean."

"Yeah, what the hell you think we out here for, anyway?"

The boy continued stroking his shotgun. His father nudged him. "Pay attention, son."

"Now I say—since the niggers ain't gonna be here no longer—we oughta take all of these young boys, and some of the old ones too—some of us old ones—and let 'em have plenty of time."

The boys in the crowd cheered.

"Why else you think we made the women stay home?" an old man shouted.

"Of course," the man said, getting down from the car, "that'll be a secret just between us men."

The cars sped through the woods. As they neared the fork in the road they saw a bright orange glow in the sky coming from the direction of the Jacobs mansion.

"What the hell!" the sheriff said, flooring the accelerator.

The road was lined with trees and they couldn't yet see the house, but as they reached the fork, it came into view. It was completely engulfed in flame. They stopped the cars and ran to join the others. They heard a woman scream. The fire raged on and she kept on screaming. When she stopped at last, the men waited, expecting to hear her voice again. Slowly, then, tree by tree, the long row of willows leading away from the house broke into flame.

"What'll we do now, Sheriff?"

"Yeah, we can't just stand here. There's a white woman and a white child in that house, burnin' to death."

The sheriff was dumbstruck. He was shocked into inactivity.

"Our niggers couldn't do this," he finally said, so softly that the deputy standing next to him could not hear him. "Our niggers are good niggers. They're just like little children. They wouldn't do this to us. *They couldn't do this to us!*" he suddenly shouted.

A man jumped up on top of the squad car. "There's something burning back that way," he said, pointing in the direction of town.

Instinctively they all looked back and waited. And then they saw what they had feared; the sky lighted up over Jacobsville.

"The niggers are burnin' our town!"

They scattered, heading back to Jacobsville, some on foot, some in cars. There was an explosion, and a tree fell blocking the road two hundred yards in front of the foremost car. And then the forest began burning. All around them Negroes were running with torches, lighting the trees.

"They're trying to burn us alive," a trooper shouted.

"The damn fools," the sheriff said. "They'll kill us and them both. Don't they know can't nobody get out of here, not even them."

He began yelling at them: "Stop! You'll kill your own people too. Stop! Crazy goddamn niggers! They're in the woods! Kill them! Kill the black bastards!" He ran as close to the burning brush as he could, and began shooting at the shadows that moved among the trees.

"Mr. Sheriff!" Josh shouted.

"Josh, boy. Where are you?"

"Over here," Josh called from behind the leaping flames.

Sheriff Pitch turned in the direction of the voice. He squinted painfully, trying to see through the glare.

"Get me out of here, Josh! Get me out of here, son!"

Josh raised the rifle the sheriff had given him only two years ago and sighted in on the sheriff's head.

"Hurry, Josh! Get me out of here!"

Josh lowered the weapon, wiped the tears away from his face. "I wish to God I could, Mr. Sheriff," he called out. "I wish to God . . ." He wiped his nose, raised the rifle again and squeezed one round that ripped through the top of the sheriff's head. He lowered the gun and started running toward town. As he ran he counted twenty explosions. Then everything was quiet except for cracking timber and his own breathing and the sound of his feet beating the ground in rapid, even cadence.

"Good-by, Mr. Sheriff," he said sadly.

When Josh reached town the jail, which stood off by itself, was the only building not burning. The white women and children who had been left behind were vainly trying to save their homes. The bank was completely consumed. The vault had been blown and looted and the big door could be seen glowing white hot in the flames. The grocery store had been emptied and the body of the grocer lay on the floor, charred even blacker than his assailants.

"Get to the lake!" Josh shouted. He grabbed two women

and shoved them gently away from the building. "Get to the lake or y'all be blown to pieces. That gas station's gonna blow this whole town to pieces. Get to the lake!"

"Josh!" a woman shouted, pulling on his arm. "Where's my husband?"

"I don't know. Everythin's burnin'. I don't know where nobody is. But y'all better get out of here. James Edward! J.D.!" Two youths appeared immediately. Josh handed one of them his shotgun. "Get these ladies and children to the lake with the rest of the folks."

The boys began rounding up the white children.

Josh ran on. When he arrived at the jail, a Negro stepped from behind the building. Josh nodded and the man began throwing kerosene on the walls. When he had emptied the can he struck a match and set the jail on fire and ran.

Josh waited until the flames had consumed one whole side of the building. Then he casually reached into his pocket, took out a set of keys, unlocked the door, and hurried inside to set his emancipators free.

About the Author

RONALD LYMAN FAIR was born on October 27, 1932, in Chicago, where he attended public schools. He spent three years as a hospital corpsman in the U.S. Navy and after his military service attended the Stenotype School of Chicago. For twelve years he worked as a court reporter in Chicago. His writing appeared in the *Chicago Daily Defender* and the *Chat Noir Review* prior to the publication of his critically acclaimed first novel, *Many Thousand Gone: An American Fable* (1965). In 1967, Fair accepted a teaching position at Chicago's Columbia College and over the next three years taught at Northwestern University and Wesleyan University. He published a half dozen books in his career, including the novels *Hog Butcher* (1966), *World of Nothing* (1970), and *We Can't Breathe* (1972) as well as two collections of poetry. *Hog Butcher* was adapted to the screen as *Cornbread, Earl and Me* (1975), starring Rosalind Cash and Laurence Fishburne. Increasingly disenchanted with American politics and culture,

Fair left the United States for Europe in 1971, eventually set-tling in Finland. In 1975 he won a Guggenheim fellowship to complete a novel entitled *The Migrants*, which did not find a publisher. By 1977 he had abandoned a public writing career to become a sculptor. He died on February 13, 2018.

The text of this book is set in 11 point Adobe Garamond, a digital typeface designed by Robert Slimbach in 1989 for Adobe Systems and inspired by a hand-cut type created in the mid-1500s by Claude Garamond, as well as the italics produced during the same period by Robert Granjon. Part and chapter titles are set in Garamond Premier, a new interpretation of Claude Garamond's font issued fifteen years later by Slimbach and Adobe and touted by typography expert Thomas Phinney as "a more directly authentic revival."

The paper is acid-free and exceeds the requirements for permanence established by the American National Standards Institute.

Text design and composition by Gopa & Ted2, Inc., Albuquerque, New Mexico. Printing and binding by Sheridan, Saline, MI.